"Thank Goodness You Found Me!"

Gabe could feel her breath on his cheek, her frantic fingers plucking at his fishing vest. It was a moment of horrible enlightenment. Her desperation was sincere, and her story too bizarre to be anything but the truth.

And it had started out to be such a beautiful day.

Undecided on the best way to console a weeping amnesiac, he commenced patting her awkwardly on the back. As he looked over her shoulder, his eyes widened as another trout jumped from the water.

"Unbe-leee-vable," he said.

"I know." She pulled back, staring at him with eyes as wide and dark as a baby owl's. "I know...it's like a nightmare. I'm so glad you came. I don't know what I would have done if you hadn't found me. I'm desperate. I'm terrified. I keep thinking I'll wake up any second and it will be over. It's crazy, it's completely crazy."

Dear Reader,

Q. What does our heroine know about the hero when she first meets him?
A. Not much!

His personality, background, family—his entire life—is a total mystery. I started to think that the heroine never *truly* knows what's in store for her when she first sees the hero. In fact, *her* life from that moment on can be likened to an adventure with a "mysterious" man. And it's from these thoughts that our Valentine's Day promotion, MYSTERY MATES, was born. After all, who *is* this guy and what *is* he looking for?

Each of our heroes this month is a certain type of man, as I'm sure you can tell from the title of each February Desire book. The *Man of the Month* by Raye Morgan is *The Bachelor* . . . a man who never dreamed he'd have anything to do with—*children!* Cait London brings us *The Cowboy,* Ryanne Corey *The Stranger,* Beverly Barton *The Wanderer* and from Karen Leabo comes *The Cop.*

Peggy Moreland's hero, *The Rescuer,* is a very special man indeed. For while his story is completely fictitious, the photo on the cover is that of a Houston, Texas, fire fighter. Picked from a calendar the Houston Fire Department creates for charity, this man is truly a hero.

So, enjoy our MYSTERY MATES. They're sexy, they're handsome, they're lovable . . . and they're only from Silhouette Desire.

Lucia Macro
Senior Editor

RYANNE COREY

THE STRANGER

SILHOUETTE *Desire*

Published by Silhouette Books New York

America's Publisher of Contemporary Romance

SILHOUETTE BOOKS
300 East 42nd St., New York, N.Y. 10017

THE STRANGER

Copyright © 1993 by Tonya Wood

ISBN: 0-373-05764-4

First Silhouette Books printing February 1993

Printed in the U.S.A.

Books by Ryanne Corey

Silhouette Desire

The Valentine Street Hustle #615
Leather and Lace #657
The Stranger #764

RYANNE COREY

loves to travel, but for the first few years of her marriage, the majority of her travel experiences consisted of trips to and from the hospital to have her children. Four boys and one girl later, she decided to broaden her horizons. Unfortunately, it seemed wherever she and her husband traveled, disaster followed. A trip to Mexico coincided with a hurricane. When they visited Hawaii, a volcano erupted. And yes, they visited San Franscico just before the earthquake.

Luckily, Ryanne has a good sense of humor. She says, "Life is entirely too serious to be taken seriously." And by far, the most important ingredient in her work is humor.

A Letter from the Author

Dear Reader:

It's sad but true—this romance writer considers "date" a four-letter word. When I was a senior in high school, I realized I was cursed. My dates were always disasters. I tried to have fun, but those magical moments I'd always dreamed about were few and far between. I remember one date in particular—would that I could forget. My older brother had asked me to go out with one of his bashful friends, who at the age of twenty-one had purportedly never had a date. I'm a tenderhearted soul, so I agreed. This fellow's nickname was "Spider." It didn't occur to me to ask my brother *why* everyone called him Spider. This was a mistake. Spider had eight arms, and he was very energetic. He tried to kiss me three seconds after we met, he tried to kiss me at every stoplight, he tried to kiss me each and every time we happened to make eye contact. If this was his first date (not!), he was making up for lost time. When he finally took me home, I literally jumped out of the car before it came to a full stop. Then I ran into the house and buried by fist in my brother's stomach.

When I met my husband, I adored him on sight, so I never took the risk of dating him. We had romantic appointments, rendezvous and get-togethers, but *never* dates. No wonder it turned out so beautifully.

Sincerely,

Ryanne Corey

One

It was a horrible thing to wake up and find a chipmunk perched on your chest.

It was balancing on her collarbone, razor-sharp claws digging into her skin through her clothes. Its beady little eyes were only inches from her face, moist and dark and busy. There was no time to wonder how she had come to be in this bizarre predicament. This chipmunk looked hostile, possibly carnivorous, and she wanted it *off*.

Blind panic ripped forth a keening wail from her throat. The startled little furry thing emitted a shrill sound like a policeman's whistle and scurried away— via her shoulder and neck. The feel of a warm wriggling body making tracks over her jugular vein multiplied her shock, sending her into a frenzy of holy terror. She wrapped her arms around her shuddering body and with her mouth wide open and her eyes bulging, she let out the scream of a lifetime. Somewhere in the middle of it all, she realized that she had a devil of a headache, and screaming was only adding to her misery.

She struggled to be calm, pressing her hands into her heaving stomach. The last gasp of panic finally bubbled out, and she slowly turned her throbbing head, relieved beyond words to see that the little monster had vanished. Thank heaven, he had disappeared into the...

Woods. The *woods?*

She gave a desolate whimper, the only sound she was still capable of. To the left was a forest of green. To the right was a forest of green. Three feet directly above her head was a weather-beaten redwood table with spiderwebs and dirt and unspeakably gross things sticking to the bottom. Beneath her was hard-packed dirt and stones.

There are some moments of confusion in life that require intense soul-searching. This was one of them. She closed her eyes and held herself perfectly still, waiting for her dumbfounded brain to explain why she might be sleeping beneath a picnic table in the middle of a forest. When no answers came, she told herself she was too rattled to think clearly. She wriggled her way off a rock that was pushing up between her shoulder blades and took a deep breath. Still, it was incredibly hard to concentrate, almost physically painful. The fiery throbbing beneath her skull seemed to go far deeper than any headache should, blocking rational thought. Her mind remained terrifyingly silent. There was no logical explanation for her bizarre circumstances. There was no illogical explanation. The heat stains on her face turned to ice and eerie chills played along her nerves. Her heart kicked up inside her chest, thumping painfully against her ribs.

She remembered absolutely nothing.

Her numb fingers closed over handfuls of dirt while she wished for a miracle that would give her back some tiny scrap of her past, what she had eaten for breakfast that morning, *anything*. The harder she strained to look into her subconscious, the more frightened she became. Dear heaven, she couldn't even come up with her own name.

A sob hiccuped from her throat, but she didn't want to aggravate her demon headache by crying. Instead, she slowly crawled out from beneath the picnic table and sat back on her heels, blinking away the sunspots that exploded in front of her eyes. She was in some sort of clearing—a small campground that looked as if it hadn't been used in some time. Nothing looked even remotely familiar. There was a fire pit nearby, filled with dusty ashes, charred beer cans and old chicken bones. At least, she *hoped* they were chicken bones. People bones were larger and less apt to be found lying about in campgrounds. Weren't they?

"I'm losing my mind," she said. No, that wasn't accurate—she had already *lost* her mind. It had completely abandoned her, taking her identity along with it. She needed help. In all the history of the world, no one had ever needed help as much as she did at this particular moment.

Slowly she climbed onto the picnic table, shaky as a custard statue. Once she was certain of her balance, she cupped her hands to her mouth and cried out for help. Again and again, facing in all directions, each time gasping and wincing at the echoing pain in her poor head. After several minutes of this, she came to a frightening conclusion. She was alone, utterly and completely alone in the wilderness.

She sat down on the edge of the table and prayed for a divine voice to call down from the bright blue sky and give her guidance. A skinny gray rabbit zipped through the clearing at forty miles per hour, kicking up miniature mushroom clouds of dust. It was a poor response to a very sincere prayer, and she decided she couldn't depend on heavenly intervention to solve her dilemma. There was no one waiting in the wings to come to her rescue. She was on her own.

Sniffing now and again, she took inventory of her assets. She had on a very nice pair of open-toe pumps that looked quite expensive, but were probably treacherous on wilderness trails. Her white silk blouse and short, wraparound skirt were drop-dead chic, but poor protection against the chilly mountain breeze tossing through the trees. Her slim gold watch was studded with tiny diamond chips, but the face was broken and the minute hand missing. Useless as well. Apparently, she had no assets.

A cloudy veil seemed to settle over her vision, dissolving the trees and bushes in a blurry green mosaic. She realized she was nearly stuporous with exhaustion. She wanted nothing more than to lie down on top of the picnic table and sleep this whole nightmare away, but she was afraid if she did, she would never get up again. No, first things first. She blinked furiously, bringing a partially overgrown path at the edge of the clearing into focus. Of course. If she was in a public campground, there must be some sort of main road nearby. She would follow the path, find the road and flag down a car. Someone would help her. Someone would take pity on her and give her food and water and make sure she received proper medical assistance.

She would get *herself* back, she vowed, or her name wasn't... her name wasn't...

She bent her head over her knees as tears tumbled down her face.

Gabriel Coulter was a contented man.

He was alone, and he liked it that way. In the bed of his pickup, he had his good old split-bamboo fishing rod with the graphite single-action fly reel, and eighteen-pocket vest, rubber chest waders and a roomy wicker creel. After a couple of hours fly-fishing at Cottonwood Creek, that creel would be filled with freshly caught rainbow and cutthroat trout. Gabe had no doubt the fish would be biting. Fate was smiling on him today. After he'd caught his limit—and he would—he would take his fish home and fry them up for lunch, then spend the afternoon tying a couple of new Olive Woolly Bugger flies. A man could never have too many Olive Woolly Buggers.

Some called him a hermit. He called himself lucky.

He parked his truck in the usual spot, on the rutted soft shoulder of a dirt road a mile from Cottonwood

Creek. It was a long walk down to the water but well
worth it. The more accessible streams were gathering
spots for amateur fishermen—usually tourists who
cast their lines as if they intended to whip the fish to
death. Gabe didn't mind going to a little extra effort
if it assured him of an uninterrupted morning's sport.

He pulled his gear from the back of his truck, don-
ning his vest, slinging the leather strap of the creel over
his shoulder and carrying his pole and waders. Before
setting off, he grinned and saluted the sticker on the
bumper of the Dodge Powerwagon: Time Spent Fishing Cannot Be Deducted from a Man's Life. If that
was true, Gabe Coulter would live forever.

Morning sunlight dripped on him like fountain
spray through the aspen leaves. The aromatic per-
fume of leaves and bark and wild mint mingled
warmly. Gabe had traveled the four corners of the
earth, but never had he found a paradise as alluring
and unspoiled as the Sawatch Mountains of Colorado. Here he enjoyed one peaceful day after another, tangling with nothing more challenging than a
wily old trout.

While he hiked down to the river, he whistled the
theme song from the old "Andy Griffith Show" and
counted his blessings. One, he had never married,
hence there was no wife waiting at home to scold him
if he decided to fish the entire day away. Two, his new
steel-shafted hiking boots were very comfortable.
Three, he hadn't felt a twinge from his ulcer in over a
month. And four, he had passed his fortieth birthday
last week, and not a single bleeding soul had known
about it.

Damn, but life was good.

Breaking through a grove of young aspen trees on a gently sloping hill above the river's edge, he paused, smugly surveying his domain. *His* water, twisting in a thick, sunlit ribbon through the shady wood. *His* guinea grass dotted with tiny wildflowers, softly packed down where deer had made their beds. *His* trees, his sky, his mountain-fresh air. And there, breaking from the water in a silver arc, was *his* trout, just begging to be caught.

He felt so free, so exhilarated, he just had to do it. He set his fishing pole and his waders on the ground, then threw his head back to the sun and let out a wild Tarzan cry, pounding his fists in a manly way on his eighteen-pocket fishing vest. Practice was paying off; he was getting as good as Johnny Weissmuller himself. He half expected a herd of elephants to come thundering through the pine trees in answer to his call.

Satisfied, the King of the Sawatch Mountains was bending to retrieve his fishing pole when he suddenly froze, a peculiar tightness in his chest.

He wasn't alone.

He felt eyes like sticky fingers all over his back. He knew he wasn't mistaken—he'd been living alone long enough to know when his precious solitude had been invaded.

He turned slowly, squinting against the sun. The guinea grass sloping to the river's edge tipped slowly in the breeze. Suddenly a golden head became distinct above the undulating green. Gabe shaded his eyes with his forearm and saw a woman sitting in a sheltered grove of aspen trees near the water, her pale face riveted in his direction. There was no mistaking the look of absolute panic in her eyes.

Bloody hell, Gabe thought, deeply regretting the Tarzan yell.

He raked a hand through his long, dark brown hair, realizing what he must look like. He hadn't had a haircut in over four months. Lately he'd taken to tying a bandanna round his forehead to keep his hair out of his eyes, but today he'd left it loose, with a blowing breeze tangling it about his face. He didn't want the panic-stricken blonde diving into the river to escape the wild-haired King of the Sawatch Mountains. All that splashing would scare the fish off.

He dredged up a charming smile—it was an effort. He was out of practice when it came to charming anyone—and called out reassuringly: "Don't be frightened—I'm not dangerous. I wouldn't have let loose with that Tarzan cry if I'd known I had an audience."

Still no reaction. She didn't move, she didn't blink. Shadows from the rustling aspen leaves overhead cast lacy patterns across her delicate features. She looked very young, twenty-one or twenty-two at the most. He couldn't imagine what she was doing here by herself. He hadn't seen another car up on the road, nor had he seen any campers or backpackers in the area.

He took a few steps down the hill, trying to hold on to his charming, reassuring smile. "You surprised me as much as I surprised you. Usually it's just me and the trout when I come up here." The breeze caught her wispy bangs, lifting them off her forehead. Gabe could see what he thought was a smear of dirt near her right temple. As he moved closer, he realized it was a bruise, a ferocious bruise at that. He could also see that her dark brown eyes were red rimmed and damp, and the tip of her short nose as pink as a bunny's. Gabe felt something inside himself sink as he realized she'd been crying.

This did not bode well for a pleasant morning of fly-fishing.

He stopped several feet away from her in the knee-high grass, observing the nervous way she worried her lower lip between her teeth. "I can see you've been hurt. Is there something I can do?"

She looked confused. "Hurt?"

"A bruise," Gabe said, touching his own fore-head. "There."

She touched the area he had indicated, then sucked in her breath with a sharp hiss. "Oh, boy. No wonder my head is killing me. I didn't realize."

"You didn't realize?" Gabe wondered who on earth had allowed this poor kid to wander around the middle of nowhere by herself. She didn't know how to dress sensibly—she was wearing some kind of a silky white skirt thing, for Pete's sake. "How could you get a knot on your head like that and not know about it?"

She made a frustrated little sound and wiped her nose with the cuff of her shirt. "I don't know."

"Did you fall?"

"Maybe. I don't know. I can't remember."

Gabe met her eyes, losing all traces of his charming smile. She sounded as if she were verging on the knife-edge of hysteria. He had no desire to deal with a hysterical woman; it was time for a calm and logical male to take the situation in hand. He brushed through the grass into the sheltered thicket where she sat, going down on his haunches beside her. "You may not remember how you were hurt," he said reasonably, "but I'm sure it will come back to you if we jog your memory a bit. Let's take first things first. Tell me your name."

"I can't."

"Of course you can," he replied, trying to keep the impatience from his voice. The sun was rising high—he was losing prime angling time. "You have to trust me, or I won't be able to help you."

"You don't understand," she muttered, knuckling her eyes. "I'm blank. I can't tell you my name because I don't remember it. I don't remember *anything!* I don't have an explanation for this bruise on my head, I don't even know the color of my eyes. I woke up a couple of hours ago and realized I had been sleeping beneath a picnic table. There was a chipmunk on top of me. He had these *teeth*, and I couldn't remember whether or not chipmunks carried rabies. I don't know why I was underneath a picnic table. I don't know why I'm all by myself out here, and I don't know why I would dress like this if I was going to be camping out in the mountains. I have blisters all over my feet from walking around in these stupid shoes." Suddenly she rose up on her knees and threw her arms around his neck, pushing her wet nose against the collar of his shirt. "I'm so happy to see you. I've never been so happy to see anyone in my entire life. I couldn't find a real road, just all these overgrown trails that were probably made by bears. I didn't know what I was going to do. I thought I would die out here. I kept praying someone would find me and save me. Thank goodness you *found* me!''

Gabe could feel her breath on his cheek, her frantic fingers plucking at his fishing vest. It was a moment of horrible enlightenment. Her desperation was sincere, and her story too bizarre to be anything but the truth. No one could make up that chipmunk thing.

And it had started out to be such a beautiful day.

Undecided on the best way to console a weeping amnesiac, he commenced patting her awkwardly on the back. Over her shoulder his eyes widened as another trout jumped from the water, the morning sun sparkling off its silver-blue scales. It was a four-pounder if it was an ounce. ''Unbe-*leee*-vable,'' he said.

''I know.'' She pulled back, staring at him with eyes as wide and dark as a baby owl's. A lost baby owl. ''I know... it's like a nightmare. I'm so glad you came. I don't know what I would have done it you hadn't found me. I'm desperate. I'm terrified. I keep thinking I'll wake up any second and it will be all over, but I don't. It's crazy, it's completely—''

''Calm down. Everything's going to be fine.'' He framed her face with his hands, to quiet her before the floodgates opened again. Looking down at her, he realized for the first time he was face-to-face with sheer perfection. Even with her nose running and a garden of bruises blooming on her forehead, she was outrageously beautiful. Her bone structure was pure and striking, breathtaking, really; her wide mouth molded in lush, sulky lines... and those slanted brown eyes, dark velvet against skin as smooth and fine as a ba-

by's. Her blouse had a deep V-neck that revealed a
tantalizing close-up of luxurious cleavage. Her waist
was incredibly small, her legs beneath the short skirt
long, smooth and brown. It would have been comforting under the circumstances to see something less
alluring, but he could find no flaw. Her body was as
perfect as her face. The lady was a spectacular and
unsettling reminder of the single lack in his life during the past two years.

She kept her melting gaze upon him, her generous
lips softly parted and quivering with emotion. She
might not know her own name, Gabe thought grimly,
but she did know how to work those Bambi-browns.
He'd bet every last Olive Woolly Bugger he owned that
she was the type who couldn't pass a mirror without
staring at herself for half the day. Once upon a time
he'd been extremely partial to beautiful women, but
it was a habit he'd managed to break. He'd also given
up hang gliding, eighteen-hour workdays and chain-
smoking. Gabe was into survival these days.

He swallowed hard and dropped his hands from her
face, trying to ignore the sudden tightness in his loins
and chest. "We're all desperate, one way or another.
Look, I'm sure there's a logical explanation for all
this. I think the best thing to do is to get you some
medical help. There's a doctor in Ophir, about twenty
miles from here. He's a friend of mine. He retired a
while back, but I'm sure he'll be willing to help us
out."

"Ophir?" She tilted her head sideways, bewilderment on her beautiful face. "Ophir?"

"Ophir," Gabe repeated slowly. "Rhymes with go-pher. It's a neat little place... has a Dairy Queen and everything."

"The name doesn't ring a bell." Then, with some apprehension, "Do you think I live there? I don't *feel* like I live in a place called Ophir."

"That's a pretty safe assumption," he muttered. He was drowning in the nearness of her. The little things were pulling at him, the feminine things—the fragile curve of her jaw, the way her wet lashes starred her eyes, her breasts softly rising and falling beneath the white silk blouse. Had it been so long? He sat back on his heels, watching her with brooding eyes and a faint pinch to his mouth. "Women in these parts don't wear heels when they go camping—they're funny that way. No, I think you're imported."

"Imported?" She stared at him. "Imported from where? I don't even know where I *am*, let alone where I've been."

"You're in Colorado." Gabe watched helplessly as she slid the tip of her tongue thoughtfully along her upper lip. His body contracted sharply, as if it were a single, hard muscle. He could smell her all around him, a sweet, musky fragrance that mingled with earth and pine and fresh mountain air. He combed back his hair and shoved himself to his feet. Children had always made him uncomfortable, and beautiful women had invariably prompted him to commit incredible follies. The pale-haired waif curled up in the grass like a wounded deer was a dangerous combination of both. Distance was the key word here. "How about

Denver? Does Denver ring a bell? Aspen? Vail? Anything sound familiar?''

"No... not really." She wrinkled her pink-tipped nose and worried her small hands in her lap. "I know Denver is the capital of Colorado. I know people go to Aspen and Vail to ski. But I don't remember anything personal. I don't remember ever being in any of those places." She swallowed audibly and her shoulders drooped. "Maybe I'm just crazy. Maybe I escaped from some remote mountain institution and now I'm on the run, living with wild animals and sleeping under picnic tables."

"Well, at least we know you have a natural flair for drama," Gabe said. "That's a beginning. And I'll tell you something else, my small sniffling friend. Your first name starts with *A* and your last name starts with *J*."

Her chin flew up. "What?"

Gabe reached down and pulled her scarf from her hair with a gentle tug. "There," he said, dangling one end in front of her face. "Embroidered initials, *A* and *J*. Personalized silk scarves like those don't come cheap. I'd say we can rule out the possibility you escaped from an institution."

Misty ribbons of wheat blond hair tumbled about her face, lifting and tangling in the sun-washed breeze. Her fingers located and separated a clinging tendril from her damp lashes. "First name starts with an *A*," she murmured. "Angelica? Adrienne?"

"Agnes?" Gabe offered, handing her back the scarf. "Alberta?"

"I think I'd know if I was an Alberta."

"Agatha?"

She frowned and looped the scarf around her neck. Definitely imported. "I don't feel like an Agatha."

"I'll tell you what," Gabe said. "It's about a mile walk back to my truck, then a half hour drive to Ophir. For that long, I'll just call you A.J. Can you live with that?"

Rather than agreeing, the young woman christened A.J. suddenly screamed, picked up a rock and tossed it with a floppy overhand into the bushes. "Did you see that? Did you see the *size* of that thing? They've been stalking me all morning! They're all over the place!"

Gabe's head swiveled, brown hair flying. "What the hell are you talking about?"

"Those horrible Chip and Dale monsters. How on earth did I end up here? I need to use a rest room. I need to wash my face. I need an aspirin." She buried her face in her hands and gave an anguished moan. "I feel like an alien. I'm sure I don't belong out in nature like this. I don't think I'd even *visit* a place like this. I know there's a good explanation. Maybe I was kidnapped from my home—a really nice place—and was left up here to die."

Gabe's lips twitched. "We can only hope." He looked down at her tousled golden head, and there was a ticklish moment when he experienced the impulse to stroke her shimmering curls. Instead he swatted at a mosquito nibbling on his left ear. He wasn't some bloody white knight; he had no wish to encourage this dove-eyed girl's dependency on him.

"Time to go," he said abruptly. "There's no sense hanging around here in this chipmunk-infested wilderness. Besides, if anyone has been searching for you, they'll probably have checked with the sheriff in Ophir. It's the only town within fifty miles. Can you manage the walk back to the truck?"

She lifted her head miserably. "If you promised me a rest room, I would crawl on my hands and knees."

"That's the spirit," he replied approvingly. If all went well, he could leave her in the competent—if somewhat shaky—hands of good old Doctor Hornbaker and still salvage a couple of hours of fly-fishing later that afternoon. "It's a fairly easy hike. You'll do fine."

She took the hand he offered and slowly got to her feet, then closed her eyes and moaned softly. "Oh, boy... my stomach. My poor stomach..."

He let go of her instantly. "Hello? Are you going to be sick?"

"No. I'm starving. I haven't eaten since... well, I can't remember when I ate last. It feels like weeks."

Gabe pulled a small plastic bag from his fishing vest. Inside was a flattened hunk of processed cheese he'd brought along to use as bait. "Here. We'll find you something more substantial when we get to Ophir."

She went after the cheese with more enthusiasm than a trout had ever shown, licking her fingers and her lips with relish. "I don't know how to thank you. I don't even know your name."

Gabe gave her a long, steady look. The inner work-
ings of his mind were fanciful and dangerous, and he
reminded himself he was old enough to know better.

He made a moody sound and turned away from her.
"Call me Mr. Coulter. I've always believed in treat-
ing your elders with respect."

Two

Ophir that rhymes with Gopher was approximately eight blocks long and half as wide. On either side of this bustling metropolis was a lumpy patchwork quilt of dry farms rolling to the edge of the wooded foothills. Everything was green, with the exception of the pastel-colored frame houses set far back on the tree-lined streets. Everything was very quiet.

A.J. sat next to "Call me Mr. Coulter" in the cab of his huge green truck, shading her swollen eyes against the noonday glare and searching both sides of the road for something that would trigger her memory. There was a circular fountain in front of the Victorian-style courthouse; six stone fish stood on their tails and spouted water straight up in the air. A small roadside fruit stand offered fresh peaches, plums and something called a Juicy Ruby Ponderosa. Directly across the street, the El Cheapy Boutiquey was having a sale on "previously loved" wedding gowns. As far as she could see, everything in this town was unusual, but nothing looked even remotely familiar.

"I remember the theme from *Jaws*," she said suddenly. "Do-do-do-do, do-do-do-do..." She looked over at the man beside her, shrugging self-consciously when he lifted one dark brow. "It just came to me," she muttered. "I don't know why. Something about this place...well, never mind."

He was quiet for a moment, braking for a slow-moving tractor lumbering across a four-way stop. Then he said, "Do you remember seeing the movie? Who you were with?"

She turned her head toward the window, fighting tears and frustration. "No. I *know* the movie...but I don't remember when or where I saw it. I don't know what to do. The harder I try to remember, the more elusive it all seems." She stared at the rearview mirror on the side of the truck, swallowing hard as a stranger with a visibly quivering lower lip stared back at her. Tentatively she lifted a strand of wheat blond hair, rubbing it between her fingers. Her brows were slanted dramatically above dark brown eyes, her nose short and straight, the color along her molded cheekbones almost feverish. There was a tiny, paper-thin scar on her chin, an injury she had no memory of receiving. This face—her face—looked as alien to her as this town she was in.

"Brown eyes," she remarked listlessly. "I wondered."

"Nice eyes," Mr. Coulter said. Then his wide mouth flattened a little, as if he hadn't meant to say that at all. "Doc Hornbaker lives just down this street. Archie's a good man. You'll like him."

"Have you known him long?"

"I met him a couple of years ago. He put thirty-two stitches in my hand when I was learning how not to fillet a fish. He'll take good care of you."

A.J. felt the pitch and dip of her heart as she heard the note of relief in his voice. It was obvious he wanted to be done with all this as quickly as possible. She gazed at his profile, her eyes burning from tears held back. There was nothing in the stern set of his lips that suggested humor or patience. His eyes were beautiful, the corners curled in a sunburst of tiny lines, the rich blue color a sharp contrast to the darkness of his skin, but they revealed precious little of the thoughts or feelings of the man within. His long chestnut hair was wild from the breeze through the open window, his harsh bronze features gilded with sun. She could picture him wearing a six-gun and sauntering into a saloon full of bad guys; she could see him dressed in a three-piece Italian suit and delivering a powerful closing argument in front of a mesmerized jury. Neither image—outlaw nor attorney—was particularly comforting.

It was all so unreal—this man, this town, this nauseating, light-headed sensation of being removed from herself. She was buffeted by questions without answers, frustrated by the complete blankness of her mind. If it needed only one thing to make the situation worse, it would be Mr. Coulter's politely disguised impatience to do his duty and get back to his trout.

He wasn't much for smiling, either. Now and again his lips would quirk in something that might have been a smile had it lived to grow up, but that's as far as it went. Didn't he realize he was quite literally the only friend she had in the world? That a little sympathy would be appreciated? It was difficult to feel at ease with a man who insisted on being called *Mr. Coulter*. She wished she could hear him laugh. She wished she could call him something warm and folksy, like Bud or Andy. She wanted him to tell her everything was going to be all right.

She closed her fist tight, feeling dangerously close to the end of her resources.

"I'm frightened," she whispered. She tried not to sound too pathetic, but it was hard. In her past life— in her *real* life—she was probably a spineless jelly-fish.

He turned his head and caught her gaze. The wind took his hair in all directions, across his cheek, tangling in his lashes. His head was backlit by the sun for a moment, casting his high-boned features in light and shadow. She caught a whisper of emotion in those haunting blue eyes, but she could only guess at the substance.

He turned back to his driving, but his hand came out and touched hers on the seat between them. His fingers curled over her wrist, squeezing lightly. And though the gesture was meant to be reassuring, the delicate pressure sparked something more—an instant awareness of his physical presence. A cold flutter skimmed her nerves as she stared at his brown fingers against her pale skin. Her throat grew tight and a startled frown furrowed her brow. She glanced up at him, watching the tense perfection of his profile. His features were composed, yet she sensed he was much more attuned to her than he appeared.

Involuntarily her gaze traversed his body. He had removed the strange bulky vest he'd worn earlier, revealing a pale blue denim shirt frayed to white at the collar and cuffs. The soft material wind-rippled gently over the tough, sculpted muscles in his shoulders and chest. She drew in a breath and held it.

"Here we are." He released her hand abruptly, clamping his fingers on the steering wheel. He turned the truck into the driveway of a white clapboard house decorated with an abundance of tangerine-colored gingerbread trim. The window boxes were stenciled with brightly colored Easter eggs and leaping hot pink rabbits. High up on the gabled roof, the stars and stripes flew proudly from the television antenna. "Good, his car's in the carport—he's home."

A.J. blinked at this startling, fanciful dwelling. "The doctor lives here?" Her attention was caught by the hand-painted sign tacked over the front door: The Main Obligation Is To Amuse Yourself. "Mr. Coulter, I really hate to bother your friend. Perhaps we should just have someone at the hospital take a look at me... ?"

He turned off the engine, then shifted in the seat and regarded her thoughtfully. "Why not? We'll drive straight to the University of Ophir Medical Center and check you into the special wing for wandering amnesiacs with chipmunk phobias.''

She bit her lip. "There's no hospital?"

"Oh, there's a brand new hospital...in Whittier, which is over two hundred miles—" he jerked his thumb over his shoulder "—thataway. Personally, I trust Doc Hornbaker completely. I'd feel better if he had a look at you right away, but it's your decision."

She didn't want to be difficult. Neither did she want to be examined by a doctor whose main obligation was to amuse himself, but it seemed she had no choice.

"Those are very interesting paintings on the window boxes," she said faintly. "Did he do those himself?"

During his thirty-five years as Ophir's one and only general practitioner, Dr. Hornbaker had used the library at the back of his house as an after-hours office and examining room for emergencies. Since his retirement, he'd torn out the built-in bookshelves and converted the room into a personal fitness center, crowding the small space with equipment he'd ordered through a home shopping channel. Fortunately, he'd kept the examining table around to use for catnaps when he tired himself out on his treadmill.

Gabe waited in the hall while Dr. Hornbaker ushered A.J. into the examining room-gymnasium. He paced slowly back and forth in front of the closed door, hands stuffed deep in his pockets, fingers curled in hidden empathy. He listened, but could only hear murmurs. He couldn't forget the way A.J. had looked at him in the truck, all eyes and heartbreaking uncertainty. It had touched an answering chord somewhere deep inside him. Two years ago he had come to this place simply because it was a long, long way from anywhere. At the time, he had belonged to nothing and no one. He knew what it was like to be alone and confused, looking for home.

He felt for her. He felt for himself, as well, because he couldn't stop imagining what it would be like to have her slim, naked body warm and willing beneath him. In his mind he saw her lips, her eyes, the sun reaching deep in her hair. He knew it was foolish, not to mention masochistic, to allow his mind to wander down this particular path, but he couldn't seem to help himself.

He stopped pacing, leaning his head back against the wall and staring moodily at the ceiling. He was no young Lochinvar, and he'd best remember it. He'd done what he could for her, and now common sense told him to leave it alone, to keep things in perspective. Mother Nature had played a little joke on the King of the Sawatch Mountains, mischievously sending a golden-haired Venus to disrupt a fine day's fishing. Mother Nature obviously knew Gabe's weakness.

After twenty minutes, the doctor passed his bushy silver head out the door and asked Gabe to join them. Gabe was familiar with his friend's idiosyncrasies. He didn't bat an eye when Dr. Hornbaker invited him to take a seat on the stationary bike.

A.J. was sitting on the examining table, her long legs dangling over the side. When Gabe straddled the exercise bike, she smiled stiffly, her wet cinnamon eyes hazy with stress. Her hair was pushed back behind her ears; her slender throat looked incredibly fragile and delicate. So pretty.

Gabe set his jaw, gripping the handlebars with cold fingers. He tried to keep his eyes averted, but they kept straying to the rounded outline of her thighs beneath the filmy skirt. *Trout,* he thought fiercely, trying to distract himself from her siren's body and soft, sad eyes. *Night crawlers. Olive Woolly Buggers. Largemouth bass, bluegills, crappies...*

"A frustrating situation," Dr. Hornbaker announced.

"Tell me about it," Gabe muttered.

"Medically speaking, there isn't much I can do," the doctor went on. "The blow she sustained to the head was severe enough to result in a concussion. Under the circumstances, a temporary memory loss is not uncommon."

"Temporary?" A.J. echoed, her reflective gaze swinging from Dr. Hornbaker to Gabe and back again. "Then my memory will return? Soon?"

"There's no timetable in cases like this. It could return within the next few hours, the next few days... I can't say. More than likely, bits and pieces of your past will come to you gradually, over a period of time. My advice to you is to simply rest and heal, and allow your memory to return naturally." He smiled and wiggled his bushy eyebrows at A.J. "It may reassure you to know that I'm something of an expert on amnesia. I watch soap operas religiously."

Gabe raked back his tangled bangs, throwing the doctor a baleful stare. "Oh, that's just dandy, Archie.

Put her mind at ease, why don't you? Make her think you're a complete lunatic.''

"Laughter is the best medicine,'' Dr. Hornbaker returned piously. "You've lived alone too long, Gabe Coulter. You've lost your sense of humor.''

Gabe.

A.J. slanted a sideways glance at the dark-haired man whose powerful, jean-clad thighs straddled the exercise bike. At least he had a first name now, though he hadn't invited her to use it. Gabe, probably short for Gabriel. He lived alone, which meant that he wasn't married. She wasn't surprised. He gave the impression of a man used to having his own way. Married men were probably more adaptable.

Suddenly she gasped, her entire body stiffening.

Gabe stood, still straddling the bicycle. "What? Are you in pain? *What?*''

"I could be married,'' she said. "I could have a husband.''

Dr. Hornbaker nodded wisely. "Married women usually do.''

"But a *husband*...'' A.J.'s voice trailed off uncertainly. It was the most incredible thought, that she could be married to a man she didn't even remember. That he could be out there somewhere, worried about her, looking for her....

She screamed, then clapped a hand over her mouth.

"Damn it, what *now?*'' Gabe was off the bike, crossing over to her with a fluid stride. "If you're not in pain, stop making those noises.''

"Children,'' she breathed incredulously. She stared at the middle button on Gabe's shirt with glazed eyes, as if she were seeing some terrible, bewildering vision. "I could have children. God knows how many children I could have."

Dr. Hornbaker rose on tiptoe, peering at her over Gabe's shoulder. "Married women often do. Of course, it's unlikely you could have more than one or two. The age thing, you know. You're just a spring chicken yourself."

"But children . . . how could I forget my children? What kind of woman—"

"You don't have children!" Gabe snapped. He couldn't believe how these two were going on, as if this were one of those bleeding soap operas Archie was addicted to. "Stop encouraging her, *Doctor*. She tends to be a little melodramatic, if you haven't noticed."

A.J.'s chin went up. "How do you know I don't have children? If I have a husband, there's no reason—"

"What makes you think you have a husband?" He tossed back his hair with an impatient jerk of his head. "Look at your left hand. No wedding ring. No pale strip of skin where a ring might have been. Odds are you are neither a wife nor a mother."

He hadn't even glanced at her hand when he'd pointed out the absence of a wedding ring. Obviously he'd noticed before. Even distracted as she was with all her problems, A.J. found this very interesting. "I could still have a husband," she said, meeting his eyes. "It's possible. Maybe I just don't wear a wedding ring."

"Many married women don't," Dr. Hornbaker agreed.

Gabe held A.J.'s gaze for a long moment, never blinking, never looking away, never giving an inkling of what he might be thinking. "You don't have a husband," he said softly, succinctly. His tone suggested A.J. would be wise not to argue the point.

A.J. wet her lips. She felt shaky inside, all nerves. The unlikely husband was dismissed; reality was a dark-skinned man with moody blue eyes and a square jaw dusted with a day's growth of beard. His controlled energy seemed to heat the small room; he rocked back and forth on his heels with a slow, deliberate rhythm. Her eyes drifted to his narrow hips, watching the slight thrust and dip as he shifted his weight.

The muscles in her abdomen suddenly knotted with shocking intensity. Her blood left her head in a dizzying rush, pooling low in her body with a fiery weight. From the waist down she was taut and stinging, from the waist up she was as limp and helpless as a baby. She felt . . . *swallowed* by him.

And she liked it.

What kind of witless woman *was* she? All she could do was close her eyes and try not to fall off the examining table.

From somewhere above her Gabe made a frustrated sound deep in his throat. "I need some air. Archie, look after A.J. while I drive over to the sheriff's office. If someone's looking for her, they'll probably have checked with Theo. With any luck—"

"No," Dr. Hornbaker said.

A.J. opened her eyes. Gabe and the good doctor were standing face-to-face. One man was smiling kindly, the other was not.

"No?" Gabe repeated in a tight voice. "What do you mean, no?"

Dr. Hornbaker spread his hands. "I mean, you're out of luck. Theo's gone off fishing for a few hours. I know, because I stopped by his office this morning to invite him over for poker tonight. There's a sign tacked to the door. Anyone who has an emergency can contact the authorities in Whittier, or go hunting for Theo up at Toluca Lake. 'I dare you to find me' were his exact words. You know how it is, Gabe, being such an enthusiastic angler yourself."

"The hell I do!" Gabe shook his head in frustrated bewilderment. "Theo is a damned public servant! He's got no business fishing the entire day away! What if someone needed him? What if something happened?"

The doctor frowned. "It's Tuesday. Nothing much ever happens around here on Tuesday. You should know that by now. And watch your language—there's a lady present."

Gabe threw up his hands. "My point, exactly. That lady happened. She needs help. She needs information. She needs—"

"Twenty-four hours of bed rest," Dr. Hornbaker interrupted. "Quiet as a mouse, giving her time to heal. She needs to sleep, it's absolutely vital. She needs to relax, and Mother Nature will take care of the rest. She'll be back where she belongs in no time."

"She needs to speak with someone who can check official reports of missing persons. It's *absolutely vital* the proper authorities are contacted, people who have experience with this sort of thing. What she needs—"

"What she needs is for the two of you to stop talking about her as if she weren't here." A.J.'s voice was strained, her cheeks flushed. It stung, hearing the two of them discussing her as if she were a nasty termite problem no one was quite sure how to deal with. She pressed her hands to her temples, blinking furiously as the room threatened to dissolve behind a shiny wall of tears. When she could finally see clearly again, she slipped down from the table, gripping the edge as the floor seemed to gently undulate beneath her feet. She took a deep breath, trying to find enough oxygen to push her sluggish brain into action. "She also needs a bathroom. It's absolutely vital."

"Of course," Dr. Hornbaker said apologetically. "Turn right. It's the first door to the left. Can you manage?"

"I'll be fine." She lifted her chin and looked at Gabe, determined to salvage some small remnant of her pride. "I'm very grateful for everything you've done for me, *Mr. Coulter*, but I don't wish to be a burden. I'm feeling much better. I'll speak with the sheriff myself when he returns from his fishing trip. Please don't feel obligated to stay with me—you've already gone above and beyond the call of duty."

A moment of silence passed after she'd left the room. Then a strange sound escaped Gabe, almost a whimper. "How did this happen to me? All I wanted was a nice rainbow trout for lunch."

"This didn't happen to you," Dr. Hornbaker pointed out serenely. "It happened to her. Try and remember that during the next couple of days."

"Next couple of days?" Gabe's blue eyes held a vivid gleam that was akin to horror. "Look, I think we're having a little problem communicating here. I'm not sure what you plan on doing next, but—"

"Well, let me fill you in. In a few minutes I'm going to run over to the Food Mart and buy crackers and a green onion cheese ball for the poker game tonight. I thought it would make a nice change from pretzels. And some peanuts—you can't have a card game without peanuts on the table. Later on when Theo gets back, I'll fill him in on the situation and have him make a few calls. In the meantime, I'm depending on you to see that our patient gets plenty of rest. Peace and quiet, that's the ticket."

Gabe wasn't a man who enjoyed surprises. In the past two years, he had done exactly what he wanted, when he wanted. His life had been free of stress, with the exception of those nights when he woke from his nightmares in a cold sweat, muscles rattling and head throbbing. Even that had become a routine of sorts. He couldn't remember the last time he had been truly inconvenienced, and he wanted to keep it that way. "You're right, Archie. The more I think about it, the more I believe A.J. would be better off at the hospital in Whittier. She needs professional people to look after her while—"

"Professional people?" the doctor retorted indignantly. "Well, I like that. What am I, chopped liver? Besides, the Little George Dam just below Whittier collapsed two days ago, washing out the bridge. If you had a television or a radio out at your place like a civilized human being, you'd know these things. You'd have to go the long way to Whittier, all the way around the lake and then backtracking through Preston. That's a six-hour drive. In my *professional* opinion, A.J. needs rest far more than she needs a long drive on bad roads."

The walls were closing in on him. Gabe could feel it. "Still, wouldn't it be wise to have X rays taken, just in case—"

"I'll drive out to your place first thing in the morning and check on her. If I see any sign of complications, which I really don't expect, I'll arrange for Life Flight to transport her to Whittier or Denver."

Gabe released a slow breath. "Archie... you're the doctor here. She'd be far better off staying with—"

"With you," Dr. Hornbaker interrupted firmly. "I'm having a half dozen of my oldest and most dishonest friends over for poker tonight. There will be no peace and quiet to be found here, I promise you. Besides, you're the only security she has at the moment. You're the one who found her, you're the one who brought her here. It's natural that she's going to feel more comfortable with you than anyone else. I know how you treasure your Grizzly Adams's life-style, but you'll just have to *bear up* for a day or two." He chortled at that, holding his ample belly and shaking his silvery head. "Did you get that—bear up? Bear?

Sometimes I kill myself. Where was I? Oh, yes—it's important she feels as little stress as possible while we sort this situation out. Look after her. See that she gets a good night's sleep, and don't feed her fish more than once a day. Not everyone has your appetite for trout. Make her feel comfortable, make her feel safe. She's had something of a shock, but she's not seriously injured. To tell you the truth, I wouldn't be surprised if her memory returns by morning."

Gabe stared at him. A muscle in his cheek worked. It all felt so wrong. Wrong, wrong, wrong. He'd lived alone in his isolated mountain home, but he'd never experienced loneliness. A.J. could change that. She was a desirable woman in every sense of the word, confusing his body with hectic urges, bringing back vivid, bittersweet memories of reckless pursuits and conquests. It made him frantic and it made him resentful. Instinctively he sensed her presence could be the beginning of loneliness.

"My mistake," he said, quite seriously, "was getting out of bed this morning."

"Lighten up, for Pete's sake. I'm not asking you to put her in your will or anything. All you need to do is play the good Samaritan for a day or so. Actually, it will probably be a healthy change for you. You'll have someone to talk to, something to talk about besides baiting hooks and tying flies. Rediscover the fine art of conversation. Enjoy the sight of a pretty young woman seated across the breakfast table."

Gabe tried to envision A.J. seated at the cherry-wood trestle table he had built with his own two hands. A table that rocked like a porch swing if you happened to rest your elbows on the edge. A table that had dips and ridges big enough to lose your bowl of oatmeal in.

He was proud of that table. He was the only one who had ever sat at it, and he hardly noticed the rocking. When he ate his dinner on his handmade table, he felt like a pioneer. Rugged. Capable. Self-sufficient.

Damnation.

"Life is so interesting," Dr. Hornbaker said, with a cherub's smile. "Don't you think?"

Three

It had been a very long time since Gabe had been with a woman. In a physical situation, in a social situation...in any situation at all. He'd lost his touch.

He slanted a quick look at A.J. She was flattened against the passenger side of the truck, chewing on her nails and staring straight out the windshield at the rutted dirt road. Her stomach was growling loud enough to be heard all the way to Toluca Lake. It was the only sound either of them had made for fifteen minutes.

"I should have bought you something to eat in town," he said abruptly. "I'm sorry...I forgot. I'll fix a sandwich or something as soon as we get to my place. It's not far now."

A.J. nodded silently, her throat constricted. She was overwhelmed with a tremendous loneliness. The kindly if somewhat eccentric Dr. Hornbaker had insisted that Gabe Coulter was "tickled pink" to be looking after her in her time of need. Gabe had nodded at all the right times, but he hadn't looked tickled.

"Just down the road here. Not far at all." Gabe started drumming his fingers on the steering wheel. He was racking his brain to make polite conversation, but she wasn't contributing. She just sat there like a bump on a log, making him feel guilty for not being able to put her at ease.

"I'm not much of a cook," he remarked, his voice a shade too hearty. "Although I've learned to make a pretty good omelet. And panfried trout...there's nothing like a freshly caught panfried trout. Do you like fish?"

She looked at him with wet brown eyes. "I don't know."

Of course she didn't know. Gabe turned back to his driving, his brows drawn together. He started to say something, then stopped abruptly and shook his head.

"I know what you're thinking." A.J.'s voice held a tremor. "You can't imagine what you're going to do with me, can you?"

He shifted restlessly on the seat. He didn't look at her, but he could see her in his mind's eye—the childish texture of her pale hair, the high flush of emotion on her cheekbones, her pouting, wayward mouth. Every part of her stirred him physically, a potent invasion of his senses. If he allowed his imagination to run wild—which he wouldn't, because he was forty years old and damn well knew better—he could give her an argument on that point.

"This is a temporary situation," he said, steering his mind to a safer path. "I have an extra bedroom, you're not inconveniencing me. If I come across as a little rough around the edges, I apologize. I haven't had much company in the past two years."

She looked at him curiously, her dark eyes round and solemn. "Why?"

Gabe blinked. He couldn't remember the last time anyone had questioned him about his motives or feelings. It made him more uncomfortable than he already was, if that was possible. "I wanted peace and quiet."

"Why?"

He felt a knot twist and yank in his stomach, a brief flare of heat from his ulcer. He never thought about the whys—not anymore. It was one of the perks of living alone—there was no one around to ask those nasty, probing questions. "Why not?" he said, his lips twisting in a parody of a smile. "There are no demands on my time here. I walk in the mountains, I fish, I spend my evenings in front of a fire with a good book.... I do anything and everything that feels good to me. Everyone should be so lucky."

"Whatever turns you on," A.J. murmured. She had a mind-boggling vision of this vital, mysterious stranger with the lean-hipped, muscular body sitting in a rocking chair, spectacles perched on his nose and a copy of *Nicholas Nickleby* in his hand. "Then what you're saying is . . . you're a *retiree?*"

He rolled his eyes, letting out a frustrated breath. "I guess that's one way of putting it. I concentrate on living instead of making a living. Are you always this curious?"

"I don't know."

Naturally not. Dismally he wondered how on earth he would manage the next twenty-four hours. Obviously polite conversation would be an effort—he'd forgotten the proper questions to ask, and she'd forgotten all the answers. What a pair they made.

A.J. cleared her throat. "You know...we haven't passed another car since we left Gopher."

"Ophir."

"Ophir. You live...in a very primitive area, don't you? Not much traffic. Just a lot of...trees."

Gabe nodded. "Beautiful, isn't it? It's amazing that a spot like this still exists in the world. Miles from anywhere. No nosy neighbors, no sidewalks, no freeways, no stoplights. You can go for weeks without seeing a single soul."

Obviously the poor man was under the impression this was quite a recommendation. A.J. wasn't sure what sort of place she called home, but instinct told her she wasn't particularly fond of the great outdoors. And Lord knew she wasn't comfortable around chipmunks.

"I'm not a forest ranger," she said suddenly, with great conviction. "I don't know who I am or where I come from, but I believe in my heart I'm not a forest ranger."

Gabe's lips twisted in the almost-smile she was beginning to recognize. "Not unless they've made a radical change in their uniforms."

Another long, uncomfortable silence.

"I know what you're thinking." A.J. leaned her aching head back against the seat. "You're wishing you'd never got out of bed this morning. I know."

"It's wonderful the way you always know what I'm thinking." Gabe felt a twinge of guilt as he heard the weariness in her voice. His eyes were troubled as they scanned her face. Her sun-washed hair tossed every which way with the breeze from the half-open window, a bright halo against her pale, finely drawn features. Her sable lashes drooped, opened, then fluttered low again, like a tired child's fighting sleep. Deliberately he lowered his voice to a husky whisper. "Maybe you're a fortune teller with a traveling carnival. Maybe you tumbled out of the back of a wagon and knocked yourself silly. Now close your eyes and rest. Relax. I promise you, everything's going to be just fine."

"You're not so tough, Mr. Coulter." Her voice was woozy.

"For a retiree, I'm ferocious."

She tried to smile at him, but found she hadn't a smile left in her. She was just so tired. Disoriented with fatigue, she slumped and gravitated to the only pillow she could find, nestling her head in Gabe Coulter's lap.

Gabe expelled a long, silent, painful breath. Without permission, his body stirred with nature's response to a woman's head nestled so near to his . . . so near. He glanced down at her; the tangled web of corn silk hair spread over his thigh, the absurd, vulnerable curve of her tiny nose, her parted lips. He listened to her breathing, so soft and quiet. Temptation whispered all around him, calling him back to bridges he'd already burned. Chaos.

He didn't know if he could bear it.

A gray veil seemed to have settled over A.J., dulling her vision, muffling sound. When the truck stopped, her sleepy brain had a quick impression of a small house built of cedar and stone, a copper roof that glinted in the sun. She was led by the hand across a deep-covered porch, ushered through a door with a pretty stained-glass window. She lost her legs the moment she saw a plaid overstuffed sofa, dropping like a stone into the soft cushions, hearing her own drowsy voice asking if she could take a little nap.

She dozed for what seemed a very short time, then suppressed the urge to cry like a baby when Gabe awakened her with a tray of food. She was no longer aware of being hungry; although it was the middle of the day, her body's craving for sleep overshadowed everything else. She ate a slightly charred grilled-cheese sandwich because it seemed to be the only way to make him leave her alone, then protested irritably when he insisted she move from the sofa to a bedroom.

He put an end to the argument by picking her up and carrying her. She didn't mind this so much, since it required no effort on her part to get where he was determined she would go. Besides, the room was dark and quiet, and smelled sweetly of pine. He set her carefully on a bed made of clouds, feathers and marshmallows; the loveliest, softest, most comfortable bed in all the world.

She managed to raise her lashes and give him a faint, sleepy smile, her hair loose and waving over the white pillowcase. "S'cuse me," she mumbled. "So much trouble..."

"Rest now. Everything's going to be fine." His quiet voice came from far, far away, but his penetrating blue eyes seemed only inches from her face. His long hair tumbled over his forehead in wanton disorder; with the last bit of energy she possessed, she lifted her weighted hand and gently stroked it away from his face.

"I love your eyes," she said.

And she curled on her side and slept.

While A.J. dozed the afternoon away, Gabe kept himself busy. He hid the dirty laundry scattered around the bathroom. He took a broom to the dusty living room floor, sweeping everything neatly beneath a bright rag rug. He brought in a week's supply of firewood, then got himself covered in soot cleaning a heaping mound of ashes from the fireplace.

You have beautiful eyes.

Like a stupid schoolboy, he couldn't forget. Her soft voice, the feel of her hand on his skin. Gentle things. As he stripped off his dirty clothes in front of the bathroom mirror, he was surprised to see a faint smile on his lips. He didn't want to smile because of her. He didn't want her having any sort of effect on him at all. He didn't want to want...anything.

And he wouldn't, damn it.

He showered, then pulled on a pair of clean jeans. He was tugging a white sweatshirt over his head when the silence in the tiny house was shattered by a woman's terrified scream.

For a paralyzed instant, Gabe was caught between shock and fear. Then he was racing down the hall, barefoot, wet hair flying in his face, mind going at light-speed. He'd left the window open in A.J.'s bedroom. Anything could have crawled in. *Bears?* he thought frantically. *Snakes? Chipmunks? Lord, don't let it be a bear.* He slammed the bedroom door open with the palm of his hand, then skidded three feet into the room over the polished pine floor before he came to a stop. "What? What? *What?*"

A.J. was sitting up in bed, one shaking finger pointing in the direction of the window. There, climbing over the sill and into the room was a tall, wild-haired creature covered from neck to ankle in a floor-length khaki overcoat.

"Get him!" A.J. shouted, jabbing her finger. "He's coming in! Do something!"

Gabe's broad shoulders rose and fell as he took a deep, steadying breath. He was grateful it wasn't a bear, but he wished he had his gun. He felt like shooting something . . . or someone.

"Damn it all to hell, Boyd." He spoke through his teeth, shaking his hair from his eyes. "Are you nuts? What are you doing crawling through the bloody window?"

"I'm practicing silent tracking." Boyd swung his legs over the sill and dropped to the floor. "I didn't think you used this room. I wanted to see if I could get in and out of the house without being seen. Didn't realize you had company."

A.J.'s jaw hung slack. Ragged heartbeats filled her throat. This Boyd person seemed to be made almost entirely of hair and overcoat. She stared at him as he raised his hand and wiggled his fingers at her, a cavernous grin splitting his rust-colored beard.

"Hullo," he said. "Sorry if I spooked you. Gabe doesn't have many friends over. Actually, Gabe never has friends over. I didn't think Gabe *had* any."

"Put a cork in it, Boyd." Gabe walked over to the side of the bed, frowning down at A.J. "Are you all right? I'm sorry about this. There's no reason to be frightened. Boyd isn't dangerous, he's just . . . incredibly strange."

"Strange," A.J. echoed, her voice breaking precariously. She wondered wildly if she was supposed to be reassured by the fact that the man who had crawled in her window was merely incredibly strange and not dangerous.

"Unique," Boyd corrected, tossing his shoulder-length head of hair with lionly confidence. "I fear Gabe is confusing my being unique with being strange. It's a common mistake."

Gabe put his hand lightly on A.J.'s shoulder. She looked up at him, blinking as if she were shaking off a bad dream. The swelling on her forehead had gone down slightly, but the bruises were blooming in a riot of color. Gabe didn't care for the painful twinge of emotion that touched his heart as he stared at her huge, overbright brown eyes. Neither did he want to put a name to it. "Like I said, Boyd is strange. If we ignore him, there's a very good chance he'll go away."

A.J. plucked nervously at the wool blanket covering her legs. "I know it's none of my business, but why is he tracking you?"

Gabe sighed. "Why are you tracking me, Boyd?"

"It's an exercise," Boyd said cheerfully. "You put on a pair of fine soft shoes like my moccasins here—" he held up one large foot for Gabe's inspection "—and you practice sneaking around the countryside on the balls of your feet. Silent tracking, just like an Indian. With a little time and effort, you can get the jump on anything and anyone—wild animals, escaped fugitives, renegade Boy Scouts—you name it. I'm still just a beginner, of course. I need practice if I'm ever going to become a true survivalist, Gabe. It's your poor luck you happen to be the only one around to practice on. It's impossible to be sneaky unless there's someone around not to see you."

Gabe closed his eyes for mental balance. He wondered how a day that had started out so promising could have turned into a fiasco with absolutely no effort on his part. Next thing he knew, he'd find an Avon lady on his front porch. He didn't want to deal with any of this, but who was asking him?

Belatedly he realized his palm was still resting on the curve of A.J.'s shoulder. He opened his eyes and gazed down at his hand against the white silk blouse; his fingers pressed into her soft skin ever so slightly. He could feel her warmth.

His body began to betray him once again. Confused, angry and embarrassed, he quickly stepped back, focusing all his fractured energy on Boyd. "You scared her to death coming through the window like that. I don't care how bloody unique you are, Boyd— next time use the front door."

"That would have defeated my purpose," Boyd said imperturbably, finding himself a seat on the cedar chest against the wall. He smiled again at A.J., cocking his head to one side. "And how do *you* do? We haven't met formally, and Gabe Coulter is too much of a hermit crab to bother with civilities. I'm Boyd Berrenger. I'm the proud owner of twenty acres of land on the west side of Soldier Creek reservoir. And you are...?"

A.J. exchanged a look with Gabe.

"She's visiting for a day or so," Gabe said.

"So you're a *friend* of Gabe's," Boyd marveled, ignoring the sulfurous glare Gabe was giving him. "An actual *house guest*. Amazing. Around these parts, the man is notorious for being a loner. You don't happen to be from Salt Lake City, do you?"

A.J. became very still. "Why would you think that?"

"I could swear I've seen you before." Boyd tugged thoughtfully at his beard. "Except I've never really been anywhere but Utah and Colorado. I was a meteorologist for KZTV News in Salt Lake City before I moved here a year ago. Any chance we might have run into each other?"

I could swear I've seen you before.

A.J. stared at Boyd, afraid to move, afraid he might see her in a different light and realize he was mistaken. She heard herself breathing, ragged and uneven. "Can't you remember?" she asked hoarsely. "I don't believe this. Can't you remember something, *anything* about me?"

"Well...not at the moment." Boyd began to look a little uncomfortable at A.J.'s obvious distress. "Please don't take it personally, I'm terrible with names. Did we work together? If you could just refresh my memory, I'm sure it will all come back to me—"

"She *can't* refresh your memory!" Gabe interrupted, raking back his hair with an impatient hand. "You don't get it, Boyd. You could have been her best friend's big brother and she wouldn't remember you."

"I'm not all *that* forgettable," Boyd said indignantly. "You know Gabe, you really have an attitude. Maybe if you got out a little more—"

"I don't need to get out more." Gabe's voice was deceptively soft. "Company seems to be coming to me these days, and they're not even bothering to use the bloody front door. But as long as you're here, try to remember where you might have seen A.J. before. It's important. Even the smallest detail could help."

"I'm falling behind here, people. Nothing is making sense." Boyd dropped his head back against the wall with a sigh, then his face slowly changed with a new awareness. "Wait a minute. That bruise on her head...was she in some kind of an accident? Did it affect her memory? Is this like...some kind of an amnesia thing?"

"You can ask me yourself," A.J. said irritably. "Just because I lost my memory, everyone thinks I lost my vocabulary. Yes, I suppose I had an accident. I must have. I woke up this morning underneath a picnic table in the middle of nowhere. I had a splitting headache and chipmunks were attacking me. That's all I know. Literally."

"And you weren't carrying any kind of identification?"

There was a sudden tightness in her throat that made speech painful. "A scarf with the initials *A* and *J* on it. That's it."

Boyd whistled softly. "You poor kid. Amnesia. Picnic tables. Chipmunks. What a *trip*. How did you find Gabe?"

"Mr. Coulter found me. He was fishing. At least, he meant to go fishing. He ended up w-with m-me." She swallowed a choking breath, sending a wild-eyed look around the room. Everything here was terrifyingly alien. Furry green things crowding every window. A meteorologist-turned-survivalist on the cedar chest. A frustrated hermit-fisherman next to the bed, simmering with resentment. Pictures of wild animals framed in tree branches on the walls. No, no, no—she didn't belong here, she knew it with every fiber of her being. She belonged somewhere—civilized.

The panic that had been simmering since she'd first opened her eyes that morning seemed suddenly to reach a boiling point, scalding every part of her body. Before her little nap she hadn't the resources to do justice to her emotions; now she was more than capable of complete hysteria.

She sniffed once, a warning. Then, with an anguished wail, she collapsed in a shaking ball of misery, head bowed into her hands, shoulders heaving,

tears running like rain through her fingers onto the
bed. She felt so young, so tormented, so *alone*. It
wasn't fair. Whoever she'd been before today, whatever she'd done, surely she didn't deserve all of this.
She started banging her fists on the mattress, each
blow flattening an imaginary chipmunk. She couldn't
stop. Her chest was heaving with choked hiccups, her
face splotchy with tears and temper.

"This isn't good." Boyd half stood, then sat down
again, giving Gabe a stricken look. "This is not good
for someone in her condition. Do something."

Gabe felt like someone had planted a fist in his
stomach. He'd never seen anyone cry like that, with so
much . . . enthusiasm. He was afraid if he put his arms
around her, tried to comfort her, she would crumble
into tiny little pieces.

"Calm down now," he said inanely to the sobbing
huddle on the bed. "This isn't doing anyone any good.
You have to stop this."

He put out his hand, touching her hair. She pulled
away. "Don't touch me. I can't stand this, I can't take
this. I want to know who I am. I want to go home."

"You certainly will," Boyd said encouragingly.
Then, because he was a basically honest fellow, he
added, "Sooner or later. Hopefully."

That set her off again. She threw herself onto the
bed, face buried in a pillow. Frantic sobs continued.

Gabe and Boyd exchanged a look. Boyd shrugged,
throwing his hands in the air.

"I know something that might make you feel a little better," Gabe said, risking a light hand on A.J.'s

shoulder. "A nice shower. The bathroom's right down the hall. There's a robe hanging on the back of the door. Meanwhile, I'll find you something clean to wear and leave it on the bed here." He waited, not at all sure if she heard him. He wiggled her shoulder gently. "A.J.? Wouldn't you feel better if you got cleaned up a little?"

She considered, her face still lost in the pillow. In a soggy voice, she replied, "I suppose . . . *hic* . . . so."

"Well, that's fine." Gabe threw Boyd a triumphant look. "We'll just let you have a few minutes to yourself, then. I'll start dinner and Boyd can . . . Boyd can go home."

"No, I think I'll stick around," Boyd said imperturbably. "I can help with dinner. I'd like to be sure A.J.'s all right. Besides, I'm hungry. You're not having fish again, are you?"

Gabe glared at Boyd, jerking his head in the direction of the door as he patted A.J.'s shoulder. In a voice entirely at odds with his expression, he said, "Just relax now. Everything's going to be fine. We're going to take good care of you. We'll see you in the kitchen after you've had your shower. All right, A.J.?"

She lifted her tear-streaked face then, staring at him with dazed misery. "All right."

Gabe was a firm believer in leaving while the leaving was good. He ushered Boyd out the door, closing it firmly behind them. Boyd ambled on down the hall to the kitchen, chatting away about his great-grandmother's battle with amnesia after falling out of bed at the age of eighty-nine. Gabe closed his eyes and slumped heavily against the wall, feeling like a survivor of a nuclear holocaust.

Or maybe it was too soon to tell.

Four

The bathroom was teeny-weeny.

Again, A.J. had a premonition, or a hunch, or whatever it was called. She wasn't accustomed to knocking her elbow on the wall when she combed her hair. Neither was there room to hang out her clothes after she'd washed them in the teeny-weeny sink. She draped her underwear over the faucets, her skirt and slip over the shower rod and her shirt over the hook on the back of the door where Gabe's robe had hung. The bathroom was filled to overflowing with wet silk.

Clad in a terry cloth robe that swept the floor when she walked, she dashed down the hall and into the spare bedroom. While she'd showered, Gabe had placed a pair of navy blue sweats on the bed, along with thick gray socks. Everything was far too large, but he had provided a diaper-size safety pin in lieu of a belt.

There was no underwear to be had, however. Fortunately, the sweats were bulky enough to hide just about everything, as long as the safety pin remained securely fastened. She took one look in the mirror above the dresser and winced. Her pale hair was drying in a static-charged curtain around her face. Her eyes were still puffy. Her lower lip quivered faintly. She knew that her appearance and circumstances merited further tears, but she was all cried out for the time being. In fact, she was starving.

She followed a fishy smell down the hall and to the kitchen. Her woolly socks made no sound on the pine floor. Gabe was chopping up lettuce and tomatoes at the kitchen table, his back to the door. Boyd had his head buried in the refrigerator.

"No, it wasn't at work," Boyd was saying. "I have a thing for blondes. Believe me, I would have remembered if a woman like A.J. worked at the station with me. Why don't you have any beer? I could really use a beer."

"Because I don't drink beer."

Boyd came back to the table with a soft drink in hand. "Where was I? Oh, yeah. This whole thing is driving me nuts. I know I've seen her before, but I can't remember where or when."

"Was it recently?" There was an edge of frustration in Gabe's voice. Even his back looked frustrated. "Or was it ten years ago when you were in college?"

"Get serious. When I was in college, A.J. was probably in grade school. Just give me a little time. I'll remember. Have you noticed this table rocks when you lean on it?''

"So don't lean on it," Gabe said succinctly, whacking a tomato in half.

"Well, you know...if you had a full glass of orange juice or something, and you happened to set it near the edge here and then leaned forward to talk to somebody across the table, you'd end up with a lap full of juice.''

"I don't drink orange juice and I don't usually have anyone sitting across my table.''

"Don't bite my head off. You really need to get out more. You have no people skills whatsoever.''

"If only I had no people whatsoever," Gabe muttered, decimating the tomato. "Then I'd be set.''

Boyd caught sight of A.J. out of the corner of his eye. He jumped off the bench, directing a quelling look at Gabe. "We've been waiting for you, A.J. Gabe's fried us some trout from his freezer—surprise, surprise. Don't you look nice in blue?''

"Boyd." A.J.'s voice was very soft, her gaze fixed on Gabe. "If you don't mind, I'd like a word in private with Mr. Coulter.''

"I predict a nasty storm front moving into the area." Boyd picked up his can of soda and lifted it in salute to A.J. "To you, brown eyes. Let *Mr. Coulter* have it. I'll be in the living room should you wish my input.''

Gabe put down his knife so he wouldn't be tempted to toss it at Boyd's retreating back. Then he dredged up a smile for A.J., inwardly wincing as he saw the mean little fists clenched beneath the too-long sleeves of his sweatshirt. Damn, she was an emotional little thing. "I hope you didn't misunderstand what—"

"I didn't misunderstand anything, *Mr. Coulter.*" The emphasis she put on the last two words was anything but respectful. She marched up to the table, her heaving breasts just inches from his nose. One finger popped out from a fist and poked him in the chest. "I don't know how long you've been out here with the squirrels and the chipmunks, Mr. Coulter, but your manners leave something to be desired. I didn't ask to be thrust into your care. I'm sorry you find it such a strain to have me around, but it's just as difficult for me. I don't know who I am or where I came from, but I *do know* I'm not accustomed to depending on other people's charity—especially when it's reluctant charity. So why don't you just act your age and I'll try not to inflict myself on you any more than necessary? When Dr. Hornbaker drives out here tomorrow, I plan on leaving with him, so your ordeal won't last much longer. Do you think you can bear up for a few more hours, Mr. Coulter?"

Speechless, Gabe could only stare at her, wondering for a wild moment if she could have been in the army. When the lady put her mind to it, she knew how to give orders.

He opened his mouth to tell her which end was up, then closed it again. He stood stiffly, knowing she was justified in her anger but hating the prospect of admitting it. One of the perks of living alone was the thrill of always being in the right, no matter the situation.

He cleared his throat. "I believe I owe you an apology."

"Not at all," A.J. said. "I'm the one inconveniencing *you*. You've made that perfectly clear."

Gabe's eyes narrowed as he met her steady gaze. "You're not going to make this easy, are you? I'm sorry if I'm lacking in . . . in people skills. I may have become a little set in my ways the past couple of years."

"No," she said, opening her eyes wide. "Really?"

"We'll see this thing through," he went on grimly, with an if-it-kills-me tone of voice. "I want to help you in any way I can. This situation isn't going to last forever, not for either of us."

For some reason, A.J. found herself looking at his hands. His posture was self-assured, his shoulders intimidating, his expression controlled . . . but his hands gave him away. He rubbed his palms nervously over his jean-clad thighs, reminding her of a teenager on his first date. Obviously he found her presence unnerving, but not because she was intruding on his precious privacy, as she had thought.

"You're scared of me," she said.

Gabe jumped as if someone had poked him with a hot stick. "Scared of you? Why on earth would I be scared of you?"

"Because I'm a woman." She said it with quiet conviction, nodding her head. "That's your whole problem, isn't it? You've been buried out here for so long playing 'Wild Kingdom,' and all of a sudden you're face-to-face with a real live *woman*. Mother Nature starts doing her thing—perfectly natural when you consider how long you've lived alone—and you panic.''

"The hell I do!''

"It's nothing to be ashamed of. So you're a little out of touch. Big deal. So you've forgotten how to relate to a woman with any finesse. That's not a problem. Just relax. Try and forget I'm a woman, and maybe you'll feel more...capable.''

"Capable?'' He said the word softly, holding her eyes. "Did you say capable?''

A.J. wondered if she might have gone a little too far. "Forget it. I was just trying to put you at ease.''

"How sweet of you.'' He studied her for the longest time, then slowly lifted his hand, trailing the tip of his finger down the side of her throat. He uncoiled a slow, suggestive smile, his summer blue eyes drifting down to rest on her mouth. "A crusty old hermit like me needs all the help he can get. It's not like riding a bicycle.''

"What's not?'' A.J. had trouble finding her voice. He was so close she could see her own reflection within the black-ringed irises of his eyes. So close his breath was a gentle whisper on her lips.

He seemed capable enough at this distance.

"Oh, you know,'' Gabe sighed, skimming his finger inside the collar of the sweatshirt. "The simple things...talking with a woman, feeling comfortable. You're right, I'm completely out of touch.'' He moved his hand to her chin, tipping it upward ever so slightly. The sugary curve of his lips filled her vision. "You'll have to be patient with me, A.J. I've lived alone so long, I have no idea how to—''

"Enough, *Mr. Coulter.*" Flushing violently, A.J. slapped away his hand. She felt as though she were melting under the subtly tempting smile in his eyes, and the caressing touch of his hand practically burned her woolly socks off. It was time to put an end to this game; her soggy knees were threatening collapse. "You've proven your point. In your day, I'm sure you were very capable."

"In my day?" A peculiar sound escaped him. She confounded him, not only with her words, but because his body was burning for what it had been denied for so long. For her, this mocking, brown-eyed Lolita who made him feel ashamed and desperate and alive, all at once. He knew he was damn well *capable* of turning her soft and hot and willing in his arms, capable of bringing her to her knees. There were ways and there were ways, and he knew them all....

But he wouldn't. He was a poor excuse for a savior, but he was all she had at the moment. He might have lost everything else in his life, but he hadn't yet lost his humanity. Hopefully.

He turned away with an abruptness that made her jump. "I think it's time to eat," he said sullenly. "Now, while I still have an appetite. *Boyd!*"

Instantly Boyd's cheerful face popped around the corner. "You hollered, oh gracious host?"

"Dinner," Gabe snapped. "Come and get it."

Still Boyd seemed reluctant to actually enter the room. "I don't want to interrupt your confrontation, uh, conversation. Are you two quite through with each other?"

Gabe looked at A.J. over his shoulder, studying her young face with narrowed eyes. She bit her lip, her heartbeat hammering furiously. Neither of them answered.

A.J.'s taste buds said no to panfried trout.

The potatoes were fine, if a little undercooked. The salad was very nice. But the fish looked, smelled and tasted like...fish. A.J. knew without a doubt that if she could remember her favorite foods, fish would not be on the list.

"You've hardly touched your dinner," Gabe commented, lifting one brow at the largely untouched portion of fish on her plate. "What's wrong?"

A.J. surreptitiously covered the trout with a piece of bread. "Nothing. Everything tasted wonderful. The salad dressing, especially. The potatoes were delicious."

"And the fish?"

"Yes, indeed," A.J. said.

"More water, anyone?" Boyd asked quickly. "No? Well, I have to say, this is a treat. I usually eat alone, some nut-and-berry thing I'm trying to develop a taste for. Being a man alone in the wilderness is a challenge, I'll tell you. Still, I don't think I've ever been happier. Being a meteorologist for KZTV never gave me a rush like tracking a deer through the woods, or setting a snare for a quail. Being self-sufficient...that's what makes life satisfying."

Gabe had the look of a man with indigestion. "Boyd, you've never killed a quail in your life. You go into Ophir every month and buy frozen Cornish game hens.''

"But I'm *capable* of building a snare and trapping a quail," Boyd replied, undaunted. "There's no sense actually doing the dirty deed unless I absolutely have to. Quails mate for life, you know. Why traumatize an entire bird family needlessly? The important thing is knowing I have the skills to survive when the big one hits.''

A.J. looked from one man to the other, feeling like she had wandered into the twilight zone. Hesitantly she asked, "The big one? The big what?''

Gabe could see that his guest was feeling a little insecure. He couldn't blame her, all things considered. Lord knew this wasn't your typical dinner party. "The big anything," he told her, feeling a twinge of pity as he looked into her wary brown eyes. Had she blinked even once during the entire meal? "Please don't take this seriously. Boyd thrives on anticipating the worst. When he worked as a meteorologist, he noticed what he thought were very ominous weather patterns. He believes the world is on the brink of major floods, earthquakes, drought—all sorts of natural disasters. Unfortunately, the folks at KZTV didn't appreciate his insight, and wouldn't allow him to air his predictions."

"I showed them," Boyd put in, winking at A.J. "I quit. I wasn't able to warn the public at large, but I could at least prepare myself. So I bought a great many survival manuals, sold my condo and moved up here. I'm living in a Winnebago motor home at the moment, but I plan on building myself a fine log cabin. Really, it was the best move I ever made. I can face an uncertain future with confidence."

A.J. smiled nervously, wondering if she was face-to-face with a weatherman who had gone over the edge. "That must be very comforting. Have you been able to predict when or where this...big one...is supposed to hit?"

"Within fifty years," Boyd said quite seriously. "First a major earthquake, then widespread flooding followed by a prolonged period of drought. Although," he added nobly, raising a hand, "I shall not be disappointed if the earth stays more or less in one piece. I'm having a splendid adventure. I wouldn't have missed it for anything. You see, that's the difference between Gabe and myself. Judging by his hostile response to my neighborly visits—and I'm really not here all that often—Gabe has come here to isolate himself from life. I, on the other hand, am happily discovering the basics of life. On the whole, I believe I'm having much more fun than he is."

"Well, thank you, Davy Crockett." Gabe stood up, stacking dishes with a vengeance. He was unnerved, and he was furious with himself for feeling that way. He was forty years old, a man who had long ago mastered the art of displaying only the emotions that would serve him best at the time. How on earth had he come to the point where a brown-eyed girl and a talkative meteorologist could so easily get under his skin? Just yesterday he would have sworn his hide was as tough as a turtle shell.

Maybe he shouldn't have moved to the mountains. Maybe he should have bought a sailboat and bobbed around the Caribbean for a few years. You didn't get unwelcome callers when you lived on a sailboat, and you sure as hell didn't stumble across any beautiful amnesiacs.

"You cracked that plate," A.J. pointed out, wondering what had set the man off. He was incredibly moody, she decided. The least little thing seemed to bother him. "You really shouldn't throw dishes around like that."

Gabe threw a pointed glance at her soft white hands, at the long raspberry-colored fingernails that were so perfectly shaped and polished. Obviously she didn't make a living working with her hands. "Somehow I doubt that you're an expert on doing dishes. Still, you're more than welcome to help."

A.J. knew a challenge when she heard one. She stood up, tossing her napkin onto the table. "Fine. Wonderful. I don't mind helping. You sound as if you think I'm incapable of loading a dishwasher."

"News flash," Gabe said laconically. "I don't have a dishwasher. I'm afraid I do these things the primitive way... by hand."

By hand. A.J. looked at the tiny sink, at the rubber dish rack nearby on the counter. A bottle of liquid soap rested on the windowsill.

And she knew without a doubt that she had never done dishes before in her life.

"Boyd and I don't mind helping," she said, although some of the spunk had gone out of her voice. "It's the least we can do for your hospitality, isn't it, Boyd?"

"It certainly is," Boyd said, getting up from the table. He still wore his overcoat; he swiped at the crumbs in the khaki folds. "Unfortunately, I have a three-mile walk back to the old Winnebago, so I'd better get moving. Gabe, has there been any mail delivered for me?"

"On the hutch there," Gabe said, taking an armful of dishes to the sink. "Three different scandal magazines and the *Sports Illustrated* swimsuit issue. For a man who wants to conquer the wilderness, you've got strange taste in reading material."

Boyd retrieved a stack of mail from the corner hutch. "One should be weaned slowly from the vices of corrupt civilization. It's a good thing the mail truck comes this far out, isn't it? Otherwise I'd have to go all the way into town for my mail."

Gabe started the water running in the sink. "We wouldn't want that. Then I wouldn't have the pleasure of—"

A sudden crash cut him off in midsentence. He took a deep, sustaining breath, then looked at A.J. over his shoulder. She was biting her lip, staring down at the shattered remains of three water glasses on the floor.

"That was the strangest thing," she muttered. "They just slipped right out of my hands."

"Unexpected things happen," Gabe said. His smile was thin. "Especially today."

"Just go on with what you're doing, I'll see myself out." Boyd started backing toward the door, silent tracking style. "No doubt the two of you are in for a cozy evening of pleasant conversation. Enjoy! I'll be in touch if I remember anything that can help you,

A.J. It's my guess you're Princess Diana's American cousin. You have the same thoroughbred look to you. Farewell, all!''

The kitchen seemed painfully quiet after he'd gone. A.J. finally risked a sideways glance at Gabe from under her lashes. He was looking at her in much the same way, blue eyes narrowed, a strange tightness to his lips.

Alone again, A.J. thought. And she felt that isolation with a startling, acute sensitivity that took her breath away. She wasn't afraid of him. It was something else that shivered between them in the small room, something that made her heart beat faster with every wordless second their eyes held.

Gabe looked away first, his shoulder muscles straining beneath the white sweatshirt as he braced his palms on the counter. "I'll clean up the glass," he said. "It's been a long day for you. You should go to bed."

"I've been sleeping all afternoon." A.J. bent down and began picking up the glass, putting the pieces in a napkin. "I'm really sorry about this. I'd like to say I'm not always this clumsy, but I'm not sure. Where's your trash can?"

"Under the sink, but there's no need—"

"I want to help. It's the least I can do."

He washed and stacked the dishes while A.J. cleaned up the glass and swept the floor. When she finished, Gabe was drying his hands on a dish towel. Finally he drew in a deep breath and raised his head, tossing the towel onto the counter. He studied her with somber blue eyes—the hint of a woman's body in the baggy sweat suit, the pale blond hair that became a fuzzy halo beneath the overhead light, the huge wool socks that drooped around her ankles. He felt desire, shame and desire, in that order. A wise man would walk straight outside and down to the lake, then keep walking until the cold water brought him to his senses.

Then again, a wise man never would have allowed himself to get into this situation in the first place.

"We could sit in the living room," he said, when it looked as if she expected him to say *something*. It was hard to believe polite chitchat had once come naturally to him. "There's a good fire going in the fireplace."

"You don't need to entertain me."

"I'm going to sit in front of the fire, not do a song and dance routine. You're welcome to join me."

Discomfited, A.J. stared at him, then slowly nodded her head. "All right. For a little while."

In the living room, he sat on the far left side of the sofa and she sat on the far right. The tiny pops and crackles from the fireplace were the only noises in the room. A.J. tried to relax, but with every passing minute her chest grew tighter. The fire seemed to generate an incredible warmth.

"You're squirming," Gabe said. He didn't look at her, just continued to stare into the fire. Subtle, heated colors from the flames shimmered over his skin and hair. "Sit back. Savor the moment."

"I don't think I'm used to just sitting...." A.J. crossed her legs, then uncrossed them. She was trying not to stare at him, but it was next to impossible. In the quiet, flickering shadows of the room, he radiated a raw and devastating sensuality. The soft white fabric of his sweatshirt couldn't disguise the hard ridges and curves of well-developed muscle. Powerful thighs pushed against the straining seams of his jeans. His beautiful hair was a tangled, glittering web-work of gold and brown, brushing his wide shoulders in the back, swept away from his face with restless fingers. Purely and simply, he was all male. A.J. decided there was something to be said for sitting back and savoring the moment.

Quietly Gabe said, "There was a time in my life when I couldn't sit still for five minutes. I couldn't even sleep longer than five minutes at a time. I didn't realize how much I was missing by not being able to relax in front of a fire."

A.J. curled her legs up beneath her on the cushions. "Still, aren't there times when you're lonely?"

"No." Not until tonight, he qualified silently. There was a woman in his life, for one night at least, reminding him with every breath she took that he had gone two years without the touch of loving hands. It was a reminder he could have done without, giving a dangerous urgency to his isolation. "I belong here," he went on grimly, as if trying to convince himself. "Everything I need, I have. It's that simple."

"And every night, you ... sit?"

"No. Some nights I go out back to the woodshop and work. I read a lot. I've been working on a topographical map of the area. I always have something to do."

It was hard to imagine. Obviously he was a complex and intelligent man, yet he'd deliberately constructed a very close, very private wall around himself. He kept his life simple, yet she knew instinctively it hadn't always been that way. Even now she could feel the repressed tension in him, the energy he was trying so hard to control.

"And you truly never wish for something more?" she asked curiously.

He turned his head then and stared at her. His gaze was heavy-lidded and mysterious. "What could you mean?" he murmured, raising one brow.

She flushed. "Well, I didn't mean . . . that."

"What?"

"You know," she replied, exasperated. "*That.* I only meant that it seems unusual for a man your age to spend so much of your time alone. Most people need companionship, conversation, intellectual stimulation. Why should you be any different?"

He shrugged vaguely and turned back to his contemplation of the fire. "We all need different things. I need the peace and quiet of these mountains a hell of a lot more than I need the flotsam and jetsam of civilized society."

"Where did you live before you came here?"

"Florida . . . Palm Beach." The answer was clipped.

"What did you do for a living?"

His hooded gaze slowly lifted to the mantel. A dusty, unopened bottle of bourbon looked out of place among the various knickknacks placed there. For a moment his lips compressed, then he looked back at A.J. with a tight smile. "It's just one question after another with you, isn't it? At least we know you weren't a tongue-tied shrinking violet before your amnesia. Maybe you were a reporter for the *Weekly Inquisitor.*"

The *Weekly Inquisitor.* The mention of the notorious tabloid raised sparklike prickles all along her skin. She knew with an absolute certainty she despised the *Weekly Inquisitor,* and everyone or anything connected with it. Unfortunately, she couldn't remember why.

Her chest lifted in a frustrated sigh. "I'd give anything to know... anything. I have these glimmers of feelings, but that's all they are. Nothing real, nothing substantial. What if I never remember? What am I going to do then? Worse yet, what if I'm a *bad person?* For all I know, my picture could be in every post office in the country. You could be sleeping with a dangerous criminal tonight, you know."

He passed a hand over his eyes, absorbing her innocent remark with a hot rush of feeling deep in his loins. Oh, she was dangerous, all right—she brought back a million memories that pulverized his heart. Spending this time with her could be more traumatic than he had feared. "I'll lock my door tonight," he said through a desert dry throat.

"Maybe you should have left me out in the woods and let the chipmunks eat me."

He looked sideways at her. "Are we feeling sorry for ourselves?"

"Yes, Mr. Coulter, we are." Her chin slumped dejectedly on her chest. "We're dog-paddling in self-pity."

"You need some lessons in fireside etiquette. You're a miserable failure at relaxing. Stand up."

"I can't relax and stand up at the same time."

"*Stand up.*"

When he shifted into respect-your-elders mode, he could be very intimidating. A.J. stood up, the sleeves of her sweatshirt dangling three inches past her fingertips. "Consider me stood up," she said.

"Very good. Now sit down—" he nodded at the floor in front of him. "There, with your back to me."

She tilted her head thoughtfully, rocking up and down on the balls of her feet. "That would put me in a perfect position for you to strangle me."

"It would." His smile was mocking. "It would also put you in a perfect position for me to rub your neck and shoulders. You need to stop tormenting yourself for five minutes. You know what Doc Hornbaker said. You have to relax and allow your memory to return naturally. Now sit."

Reassured that he had only her best interests at heart, she positioned herself Indian-style between his legs, with her back resting against the sofa. His thighs cradled her shoulders on either side. She felt warm and safe and comfortable, more so than at any time throughout this entire wretched day. She raised her hands, lifting her hair off her neck and brushing it over one shoulder. And waited. "Mr. Coulter?"

"Uh-huh" was all the reply that he gave to her. He closed his eyes, inhaling the sweet scent of her skin, listening to the soft, narcotic rhythm of her breathing. He was consumed by her physical presence, hopelessly, utterly swallowed by her. Allowing himself to get this close to temptation was sheer insanity, but he wasn't going to think about that now. He needed this. He felt her all along his body, felt her stirring and warming him deep in his skin and bones. He set his jaw and swallowed hard, lifting his hands and beginning a slow, light massage of her shoulders. "Just as I thought," he muttered. "Your muscles are tied in knots. Breathe deeply."

A.J.'s head slowly tipped forward. "Mmm. That feels nice. Very relaxing."

Gabe hardly heard her. His eyes were focused on the fragile indentation in the middle of her neck. He could imagine his lips there, imagine the tip of his tongue tasting her musky skin. His hands methodically continued their massage, but his mind drifted into dreams. He saw himself taking her here, now, her naked body stained with fire colors, her luscious mouth shining wetly. And in his fantasy she was wild and uninhibited, wanting and willing to try anything he asked of her. She was completely submissive, giving him everything he craved, opening herself to him with a delicious siren's smile. . . .

"Mr. Coulter?"

Her husky voice brought him back to reality. "Yes?"

"What are you doing?"

Hell and damnation. Somehow his hands had slipped beneath the collar of her sweatshirt, his fingers resting above the burgeoning curves of her breasts. He could feel her heartbeat in his fingertips. He wanted to take her into his arms, to hold her warmth and softness against him like a bedtime doll. Instead he took his hands away, his throat thick with longing. "It's late. Go to bed, A.J."

She met his intense gaze over her shoulder, still feeling the touch of his hands on her bare skin. She wet her upper lip with the tip of her tongue. "I'm not sleepy."

Softly, he replied, "Oh, yes you are."

The message was unmistakable. A.J. got to her feet—strangely euphoric, apprehensive, confused. She looked down at Gabe, staring at the line of his jaw, the boyish, glittering tangle of his hair. She touched her forehead as if feeling dizzy.

"That felt good," she said, so softly he had to strain to hear.

He took a moment to reply. "I'm glad the massage helped."

She pulled in a shaky breath and turned away. "I wasn't talking about the massage. Good night, Mr. Coulter."

Five

---

*R*ock music...?

Dear Lord, no. It couldn't be. Gabe thrashed around in bed, pulling his pillow over his head. There was no rock music in paradise. Just the song of birds and the gentle breeze through the aspen trees. This was just a horrible, terrible dream. It would go away if he closed his eyes and prayed hard enough.

But it didn't. If anything, it seemed to grow louder. He sat up in bed, grabbing his watch from the bed-side table. Eight o'clock. Eight o'clock in the bloody morning and electric guitars and bass drums were jamming in his kitchen.

He *hated* rock music.

He threw the covers off the bed—and halfway across the room—and he got up, grabbing a robe from the closet as he passed. His home, his sanctuary, his oasis of peace had been violated by the screeching, abominable monster he'd thought he had rid himself of forever.

The King of the Sawatch Mountains wanted someone's head on a platter. A young blond amnesiac would do.

She didn't hear him come into the kitchen. She couldn't have. The entire room was vibrating with metallic pandemonium. A clock radio Gabe had never seen before was blasting from the kitchen counter. A.J. was standing in front of the stove, hips and feet doing wondrous things in time to the music. She wore a pair of jeans he recognized as his own, cinched around her narrow waist with her silk scarf. She also wore one of his favorite chambray shirts, knotted and tied at the midriff, sleeves rolled to elbow-length. Her hair was bobbed up in a bouncing, flyaway ponytail with something that looked suspiciously like dental floss.

She looked absolutely ridiculous. She looked absolutely beautiful. She was soft and pretty and feminine, a bright-haired mirage with dancing bare feet. Staring at that rounded derriere undulating from side to side, Gabe forgot he was being assaulted by demon rock music. Other sensations assaulted him. Bone-melting pleasure. Wide-eyed shock, like he'd suddenly found himself teetering on the crumbling edge of a cliff. A deep, burning pain in the cold clutter of his heart, because it was all coming back to him like it was yesterday—all the old feelings, all the urgent, terrifying needs. Just like that.

"Help," he muttered hoarsely.

She didn't hear him. She couldn't have, yet something must have alerted her to his presence, for she suddenly spun on her heel and smiled at him. "Good morning, Mr. Coulter. I'm going to fix French toast for breakfast just as soon as I figure out how to light this strange-looking stove without blowing us both to kingdom come. If I ever knew how to cook on a gas range, it's not coming back to me. Oh, well. It's the thought that counts."

Gabe could barely hear her over the music. His eyes were on the soft tendrils of hair drifting about her face, the childlike flush in her smooth cheeks. She was a bright, magnetic presence in a room that had never seemed so warm or so welcoming.

He closed his eyes. He could feel the uneven rise and fall of his chest as he tried to control the rhythm of his breathing. After a moment, he walked over to the radio on the counter and flicked it off. The silence that followed seemed ten times louder than the music had been. He was almost sorry he'd turned it off.

He cleared his throat, trying to bear in mind how bloody irritated he was. "I wasn't aware I had a radio here."

"I found it in the closet in my room, way back on the top shelf. Maybe the former owner left it here?"

"It's been two years since I heard music like that. Two wonderful years."

A.J. stared at him, biting her lip. "Oh. I get it. You don't like music."

He lifted one eyebrow. "Not nearly as much as I like peace and quiet, especially at this hour of the morning."

"But *so much* peace and quiet," A.J. pointed out in what she thought was a reasonable voice. "It's got to get on your nerves. I couldn't believe the utter, deathly silence when I woke up this morning. It gave me the willies. I opened my window, and do you know what I heard? Birds, nothing but little birds. It wasn't *natural*."

"Call me crazy. I think the sounds of nature are sort of natural."

"You're not exactly a morning person, are you?" A.J. tilted her head sideways, wrinkling her nose. "Do you always get up on the wrong side of the bed, Mr. Coulter?"

Gabe let out a slow, deep breath. "Not usually. Then again, I usually don't wake up to a rock concert in my kitchen, either."

A.J. scuffed her bare foot along the floor. "I may have had it turned up too loud."

"A little," he said with irony.

She looked up through her tangled bangs, judging his mood for a moment, then relaxed enough to allow an impish smile to blossom. "Believe it or not," she said, with the air of someone imparting a great piece of wisdom, "you're going to miss me when I leave you, Mr. Coulter. Your precious peace and quiet won't be nearly as interesting and entertaining as I am."

It was a teasing attempt to distract and placate him, Gabe knew. Somewhere in her subconscious, A.J. was very familiar with her own devastating charms and just how to use them to her best advantage. She simply had no idea she was playing with fire.

He set his jaw and told himself he could handle this; he really could. He was a grown man, not an inexperienced adolescent with raging hormones. He managed a tight smile, staring just over her shoulder at the bright blaze of sunlight that filled the window. "Something tells me you're feeling a little better this morning."

"I couldn't believe how well I slept last night," A.J. agreed. "And this morning when I got up— Oh, by the way, I found these clothes in the dryer in the laundry room. I hope you don't mind my borrowing them. I rinsed my skirt and blouse out in the sink last night, but they're not quite dry yet. Where was I? Oh, when I got up this morning, I remembered something. It came to me just like that, out of the blue."

A strange feeling took Gabe in the stomach. "What?"

She tossed her ponytail and gave him a smug smile. "I absolutely adore French toast. It's my favorite thing in the whole world. If I remembered that, other things are bound to start coming back to me, don't you think?"

"That's what Doc Hornbaker said," Gabe replied tonelessly. Which was exactly what he wanted, to be rid of his unexpected guest and all the emotional and physical upheaval she caused. Soon he would have his precious solitude back, his insulated, undemanding existence.

Soon. An odd tightness seemed to constrict his heart for a bittersweet moment. He caught himself staring at her, his gaze riveted on the full, blatantly sensual curves of her mouth. The edges tipped up when she smiled, pushing a dimple into one cheek. *So beautiful,* he thought. While his eyes took her in, his senses registered the soft, noiseless movement of white curtains at the open window, the smell of summer sun mingled with the sweet scent of a woman's skin and hair, the almost tangible warmth of a smile. Companionship. Life, feeling, awareness. It was all there in the room with him; for the first time in two years, it was all there.

He lowered his eyes and looked away. "Which reminds me, our poker-playing doctor friend said he'd be visiting us this morning. I'd better get dressed."

"You do that," A.J. said. "Meanwhile, just tell me where the matches are and I'll do a little experimenting with this stove. It will be very interesting discovering what I can and can't do."

"Not a chance," Gabe said. "If you haven't noticed yet, you tend to be a little accident-prone. The thought of you playing with matches around a gas stove makes my blood run cold."

A.J. wrinkled her little nose. "You have no adventure in your soul, Mr. Coulter."

"One of the perks of middle age," Gabe replied. "Sanity. Go sit outside on the porch swing and listen to the unnatural birds. Breakfast will be on the table in twenty minutes."

Frowning, A.J. pursed her lips and blew her bangs out of her eyes. "I don't want to feel useless. I want to feel worthwhile."

"Believe me, not blowing us both to kingdom come will be very worthwhile." Gabe walked to the screen door leading to the back porch and held it open. "Besides, relaxing on a porch swing on a beautiful summer morning is not being useless. It's a very important, very rewarding activity. It took me a long time to discover that."

But holding the door open for her had been a mistake. Holding the door open meant she would have to move past him—which she proceeded to do—her shoulder brushing his chest, her flyaway ponytail tickling his nose, her soft, sweet fragrance drugging him like morphine. His brain shut down; his body took over. Nerve endings jerked, muscles tightened, his lungs spasmed. He had to bite his lip to keep from groaning out loud when she paused in the doorway, giving him another of her killer smiles from a paralyzing distance of six inches.

"Just one more thing," she said ingeniously. "Since we've just spent the night together—in a manner of speaking—and I *swear* I still respect you, don't you think it would be nice if I called you Gabe instead of Mr. Coulter?"

Emotionally, Gabe felt like he had suddenly fallen on his knees. He couldn't move, couldn't even blink. All his awareness was focused on her perfect face, her husky voice, the luscious body that would drive any strong, confident man to reckless things. Let alone a broken, lonely recluse without dreams or direction.

He continued to hold the door open for her, wishing with all his heart she would stop looking at him with that open, teasing tenderness. He said nothing. If he had, he would have said too much.

"You're a tough proposition, Mr. Coulter." A.J. sighed, her shoulders lifting with a resigned shrug. "You weren't by any chance an English teacher, were you? I remember an English teacher I had once named Mr. Denby-Smith *'Sir.'* He turned purple if he thought he wasn't receiving the proper respect from . . ."

Her voice trailed off. She stared at Gabe, her mouth falling open. Her hands went to his shoulders, grasping the lapels of his terry cloth robe. "Did you hear me? Did you hear that? I remember Mr. Denby-Smith. I remember sitting in a classroom . . . I don't know where . . . and listening to this man drone on and on in this horrible monotone . . . Mr. Denby-Smith! I *remember* him!" She paused for breath, her eyes growing wider as flashes of memory came and went. Trying to stay awake during a lecture. Wearing a uniform, a white blouse and black pleated skirt. "It was a private school," she said. "I went to a private school and I hated the uniform I had to wear. I remember sitting there in this awful, high-necked blouse, feeling like I was choking while Mr. Denby-Smith lectured for hours on end. I can see his face so clearly, just like it was yesterday."

The beginning of the end, Gabe thought with a strange, quiet clarity. She remembers, she leaves my life and goes back to her own. He watched her moodily through shuttered lids, his mouth taut. "That's good." His voice was low. "Things are beginning to come back to you now, just like Doc Hornbaker said. What else do you remember?"

A.J. frowned, feeling a faint throbbing at the base of her skull. She couldn't push past it, couldn't grasp the memories that were so tantalizingly close. Her eyes grew moist. "Just...just that. I can't connect that memory to anything else. It's clear, it's real, but everything else...it's all just barely out of reach."

"Don't push it." Gabe dropped his hand from the screen door, letting it close with a soft creek. She wanted comfort; she was leaning into him, helpless and innocent, her forehead burrowed against his chest. Gently he placed his hands on her back, rubbing in soft, shaky circles. He closed his eyes. "It will all come back to you when the time is right. Don't push it."

A.J. smiled tearfully, her fingers working restlessly on the lapels of his robe. "You can't tell me you're not as anxious as I am for my memory to come back."

He made a husky sound, his hands stilling on her back. It felt like he was suffocating, to be this close to her. And she didn't know, she had no idea his body was growing ready for her, his mind was spinning erotic fantasies at the speed of light. He was a scoundrel. He was a lecher.

He never wanted to let go.

"I really am sorry I've been such a nuisance," she said, her lips curling ruefully as she tipped her head back to look into his face. "I guess you'll throw yourself quite a party when I leave today."

"Today?" His eyes narrowed. He kept a check on himself, just barely. The tender roundness of her breasts nestled innocently against his chest, making him almost violent inside. His whole being reached out for her, yet he didn't move a single muscle. "What do you mean, today?"

Something in his voice made her lose her smile. "Just that I told you I would leave with Dr. Hornbaker today. We both know you don't want me—"

"Want you?" The words came out a little fractured, almost pleading. His hands moved to frame her face, the tips of his fingers stroking the delicate plane of her cheekbones. He heard her indrawn breath, saw a slow, wondering light come into her liquid brown eyes.

"Want you," he said again, so softly she could barely hear.

Like an instant fire, it came to life between them— an intense physical awareness of one another. For her, the boyish way his too-long hair tangled over his brow, the sweet play of chest muscles visible between the V-neck of his robe, the sleep-creases still evident on one cheek. For him, the precious, feminine things—the glitter of sun on her absurdly long lashes, the childish curve of her upper lip, the soft warmth of her body against his. Neither of them spoke, but the silent seconds they stood together were precarious and revealing.

Gabe shook his head faintly, denying...what? He didn't know. He dropped his hands, leaning back weakly against the wall. She didn't move. He really wished she would.

"Mr. Coulter." Her voice was soft. She made his name sound like a prayer, or a sigh. She wasn't looking at him like he was an English teacher, or even a tough proposition. She was looking at him like she'd

"I'm forty years old," Gabe said. As if that had anything do with anything.

A.J. grinned. "Well, maybe you'll get better at tables and porch swings when you get a little older. In the meantime, we could enjoy ourselves building a very fine tree house."

"We?"

"Well, I don't know how long it will be before Doc Hornbaker arrives, but I can help while I'm here. I have a crystal clear picture in my mind of the perfect tree house. If you follow my directions, it should take shape in no time at all."

"Are you trying to tell me," Gabe said slowly, "you've *remembered* this particular talent? I'm supposed to believe you're some kind of tree house specialist?"

"No, I'm not." A.J. sighed regretfully. "I'm pretty sure I don't know one end of a hammer from the other, but I've got a very good imagination. I can tell you exactly how it should look. I can even draw you a picture. You won't be sorry, I promise. A tree house is a very useful thing. I've wanted one all my life."

"You don't remember your life," Gabe pointed out.

"I remember this," A.J. insisted. "I know I've always wanted a tree house. And I know we could build something really great, a masterpiece of tree dwellings. You can provide the manual labor and I'll provide the creative input."

He gave her an arrested look. "You are by far the strangest person I have ever met in my life. I mean that sincerely."

"Thank you." She smiled at him with serene brown eyes. "I'll take that as a compliment. We'll get started on our tree house right after breakfast."

"I'm forty years old."

"You keep saying that. Do you have some kind of fixation with your age?"

"I'm too old to do anything so asinine as to spend my morning in a tree. I'll take you fishing."

"I think not. First, you have to kill an innocent worm, then comes the poor fish . . . no, building a tree house is much less violent." Her beautiful face warmed into a vision of friendly mischief. "Besides, it will give you a permanent memento of my visit here to Gopher."

His shuttered gaze played over the silk of her lashes and brows, the sun-washed halo of her hair. "*Ophir*. And I won't need a memento. You're unforgettable."

"I believe I'll take that as a compliment as well," she said judiciously. "Do you have a pair of old sneakers around? I don't think I want to try climbing a tree wearing heels."

"You won't be climbing a tree."

"I can't instruct you if I'm not up there with you."

"I won't be climbing a tree, either."

"Do you have an extra hammer?"

"You're not listening to me."

Mr. Coulter, A.J. noticed with amusement, was getting a little red around the ears. "Of course I'm listening to you. You're my host. It would be very rude not to listen to you. Why don't we get started on the French toast? I'm starving."

"*No tree house.* Stop smiling. You're crazy if you think you can smile me into something so stupid."

Her smile disappeared instantly, as ordered. "I have a temporary memory loss, Mr. Coulter. I'm not crazy. I would never try to persuade you to do something you didn't want to do."

"You couldn't if you wanted to. You might be accustomed to charming anything you want out of everyone you meet—that's just a hunch, mind you—but this time you're out of luck."

"Yes, sir, Mr. Coulter. Whatever you say."

"Good. Fine."

"Do you have an extra hammer?"

It was definitely her first tree house.

A.J. hadn't the faintest idea how to begin. She sat on a chair in the shade of the big old tree, offering a volley of suggestions that were highly creative but architecturally impossible. Finally Gabe told her to put a cork in it and watch a master at work. A.J. grinned and folded her hands in her lap, observing the creation of the finest tree house since Tarzan met Jane.

It took about an hour for the first floor to be completed, a somewhat uneven octagon that circled the massive tree trunk almost twelve feet above the ground. After Gabe had constructed a sturdy wall on all sides, he allowed A.J. to climb up and observe the proceedings firsthand. Every convenience was considered. A second story was added, large enough for one person to stretch out full-length, and christened "the penthouse." A rope ladder was built in addition to the wooden steps nailed up on the side of the tree, to ensure smooth traffic flow. A small wooden crate was brought up to use as a picnic table, and the penthouse was furnished with an old bunk bed mattress and a fuzzy red wool stadium blanket. A.J. went back inside the house and rummaged about for finishing touches, returning with a small plastic fern for the picnic table, a couple of striped throw pillows for the penthouse and a Welcome Friends mat that was neatly placed at the grassy base of the tree. Tarzan himself, she told Gabe, would have been green with envy.

Gabe rather thought she was right. He was sitting cross-legged in the penthouse surveying the fruits of his labors. A.J. was on the ground below, whistling cheerfully while she pulled milkweeds from around the tree. Her dental floss had gone the way of the wind some time before; her golden hair tumbled in sun-gilt clouds around her face. Her whistling was more air than sound, but the picture she made more than compensated.

"Now what do you want me to do?" Gabe called down to her. "Plant a little flower garden? Put up a mailbox? How about a white picket fence around the tree?"

A.J. sat back on her haunches and squinted up at him through sun-dappled leaves. "Don't pretend you didn't enjoy working on this every bit as much as I did."

He groaned loudly, more for effect than anything else. "What are you talking about? I'm the one who did all the work."

"But I had the inspiration. You would have never thought of this without me. You would have spent your entire day fishing, and what would you have had to show for it when you were done? Nothing.''

"Sometimes I actually catch a fish," Gabe murmured.

"Speak up. I can't hear you."

"Never mind." At some point during the building of this absurd tree house which had absolutely no purpose whatsoever, Gabe had found himself in a damned cheerful mood. It didn't make sense, but there it was. He liked sitting in his lofty perch above all and sundry. He liked being able to see all the way to the paved highway in one direction and as far as the reservoir in the other. He liked listening to A.J. try to whistle, he liked the way she winced and yelped in sympathy when he hammered his thumb. He liked the way she waddled in his too-large sneakers, the toes stuffed with paper towels, and he liked the way she carried wood from the workshop one little piece at a time.

He liked not being alone.

He gazed down at her like a cat watching a canary. Thinking. Wishing. Then his dark lashes lowered and he tipped his head back against the tree. He best stay right here, high above temptation. He wasn't feeling particularly noble right now, or even responsible. With his eyes closed, he could see himself seducing her, bearing her down in the wild grass and taking everything he wanted so badly. The current had been humming between them all morning long: every time she'd looked at him, he had seen the awareness in her eyes. She knew what she did to him. Worse yet, she wasn't afraid of it, either. He had the most unnerving sensation that she was simply... waiting. No one should be that self-assured at such a tender age, he thought resentfully. It wasn't fair. He was forty years old and smothering in adolescent angst.

A.J.'s voice interrupted his reverie. "I think you have a visitor, Mr. Coulter."

Gabe's eyes snapped open. Doc Hornbaker, he thought, sitting bolt upright and cracking his forehead on a low-hanging branch. He's found something out—who she is, where she belongs. He'll take her away. *Not yet, not yet.*

He looked over the treetops, seeing a cloud of dust puffing up the dirt lane. His thundering heart slowed abruptly as he recognized the wheezing rumble of Roy Cobb's mail truck. "It's just the mail," he said, trying to keep the relief out of his voice. "He never comes all the way to the house—he'll drop it off at the box down by the front gate."

A.J. stood up, brushing her hands off on her jeans. "Want me to go pick it up for you?"

"There's no rush," Gabe said, not wanting her to leave his sight. "All the mail delivered here is usually for Boyd, anyway. He subscribes to every scandal rag in the country. Then there's Log Home Quarterly, Backwoods Digest—"

"I need to stretch my legs, anyway." A.J. wiggled her fingers at Gabe, then flashed him a sudden grin. "Have I told you how cute you look playing in your tree house? No one would guess you were a day over thirty-five."

He dropped a handful of leaves on her head. "Go fetch the mail, then. I'm staying up here where I feel superior."

Still smiling, A.J. followed the gravel path that dipped along a chinked stone wall toward the road. In a moment she was out of sight from the house, walking in the shade of an overgrown hedge heavily laden with huge, dark berries. She paused long enough to pop a juicy berry into her mouth, decided it tasted too delicious to be poisonous, and ate several more. Then, tripping occasionally over her clown shoes, she continued down to the front gate where a barn-shaped wooden mailbox was perched on a carved post that leaned like the tower of Pisa. Another of Gabe's homemade treasures, A.J. thought, pressing her fingers over a smile. Funny—from the looks of him, his cynical, hard-edged features and knowing blue eyes, one would never guess he would find such satisfaction in the simple things in life. He was an enigma to her, a contradiction upon a contradiction. The more she discovered about him, the less she felt she understood him... and the more she wanted to try.

There were several pieces of mail stuffed in the mailbox; as Gabe had predicted, all were addressed to Boyd Berrenger. A newsletter titled "Living Off The Country," a couple of advertising supplements, an L.L. Bean catalog and the latest issue of The *Weekly Inquisitor*. She wrinkled her nose at the scandal magazine, barely suppressing the urge to stuff the wretched thing back into the mailbox. The headlines were ridiculous, incredible. "Loch Ness Monster Gives Birth to Twins" was certainly an eye-catcher, with an accompanying photograph showing the legendary monster swimming with what appeared to be two Vienna sausages. Another headline titillated with "Man-Eating Heiress Leaves Fiancé Number Five in Pieces! Inside Scoop on Page Six."

It was laughable, it really was. A.J. shook her head in disgust, tucking the mail under her arm and starting back up the walk toward the house. How did these publications get away with such things? They had absolutely no regard for the truth. Boyd Berrenger should have his head examined if he actually believed everything he read. . . .

Fiancé Number Five.

A.J. froze on the path, staring straight ahead at nothing. She heard the deafening rush of blood through her ears, and the demon headaches had sprung up again from nowhere. *Fiancé number five* . . . those three simple words cut through the fog and mist screening her memory like a knife, leaving her stinging and shocked. She had a sudden, baffling image of a dark, angry face, accusing words, a stinging hand across her face. *Liar . . . tease . . . damned little slut . . .*

Her sluggishly functioning brain was slow to catch up with her body's awareness. Her heart was pressing hard against her chest, crowding her lungs, and her skin was icy cold and prickling. Emotions rolled through her like thunder, jumbled and confusing. Panic. Despair. Loneliness. Anger. Nothing made sense, it all swirled around her like dry leaves in a windstorm. She knew she was coming back into the world, into reality, and she didn't like it. It was going to hurt.

She sat down abruptly, right there in the middle of the path. The mail went scattering every which way, except for the *Weekly Inquisitor,* which tumbled into her lap. She stared at it the same way she would have stared at a snake had one slithered over her knee and curled up in her lap. Oh, yes . . . it was going to hurt.

She turned one page at a time, very slowly. The photograph on page six jumped out at her in blinding, full color. A man and a woman dancing in some sort of nightclub. He was very tan, with wavy black hair that tumbled around his face in a wild mane. He wore tight jeans and a beaded vest over a white T-shirt. She had luminous blond hair and dangling diamond earrings that brushed her bare shoulders. Her clingy, red sequined minidress left little to the imagination. The caption below the picture was in bold block letters. Billion Dollar Baby Angel Conaught and Heavy Metal Guitarist Corwin Slade in Happier Days at L.A.'s Trendy Club Rascals. After a Five Week Engagement, Fifth Fiancé Is History, This Angel . . . Isn't.

The world around A.J. seemed to have gone deathly quiet. She couldn't even hear those unnatural birds she'd complained to Gabe about. She touched the laughing face of the girl with shaking fingers. "Me," she whispered. "It's me. . . ."

The article accompanying the photograph was short and anything but sweet. "Sexy Angel changed her mind yet again last month, dumping rock star Corwin Slade after wearing his ring only five weeks. He joins a notable list of changeable Angel's has-beens, including Robert Asker, a Pulitzer Prize-winning playwright twice her age, and Donny Racine of the Denver Broncos. Slade is rumored to be devastated, and is threatening to sue the notorious heiress for breach of promise. Sources sympathetic to Angel cite her grief over the recent death of her father, billionaire industrialist D. Quinn Conaught, as a contributing factor to the breakup. What then, the *Inquisitor* wonders, contributed to the four previous short-lived engagements? Angel Conaught was unavailable for comment. Angels usually are."

A.J. sucked in a gasping breath that had been a long time coming. Her mind was reeling. Angel Conaught. Her name, her face, her follies, right there in front of her. She had flashes of memories one after another, disconnected and hazy but all very real. Her heart knew the truth. She was Angel Conaught. Her middle name was—she strained to recall, then it came to her out of the blue—Jordanna, after her father's mother. The scarf threaded through the belt loops of Gabe's jeans had been a present from a friend at boarding school. On that same birthday, her father had sent her flawless, four-carat, pear-shaped diamond earrings. A gift too formal, too adult for a sixteen-year-old to appreciate. She'd hidden them away in her sock drawer and written her father a polite thank-you note.

Her father. She closed her eyes, curiously devoid of any feeling, any impression of heartbreaking grief. She felt only...emptiness. She recalled standing at the graveside, wondering how to say goodbye to someone she never really knew.

"I was getting worried about you."

Gabe. A.J. made a choked sound and quickly closed the newspaper, then gathered up the rest of the mail. She was moving automatically, knowing only that she didn't want him to see who and what she was. Not until she could make some sense of it all, not until the memories fell into some chronological order and she was able to summon the emotions to go with them. She had to be sure. Dear heaven, did she really want to be that woman? She didn't feel like Angel Conaught. She felt like A.J., a defenseless orphan of the storm who didn't much care for fish and tied up her hair with dental floss and loved tree houses.

"I tripped," she said, her voice coming out a little hoarse. "Dropped the mail. Sorry. It's all dirty, I'm afraid. Boyd won't like this, will he? I've ripped the cover of his L.L. Bean catalog. I'm sorry."

Gabe knelt down beside her, lifting her chin with his hand. "Hey, calm down. Boyd's junk mail is not a big priority in my life. Are you all right?"

She'd never seen such a gentle, concerned expression on his face before. She wondered if he would look at her that way when he really knew her. "I'm fine," she said miserably. She couldn't make the terrible dull pain in her chest go away. She needed time alone, time to think. "I think I'm just . . . tired. Maybe I overdid it this morning."

"There's no maybe about it." Gabe helped her up, touching her hair, her shoulder. He felt damn helpless, and more than a little stupid. He shouldn't have

allowed her to do so much, shouldn't have let her talk
him into building that idiotic tree house. Her dark eyes
looked like deep shadows against her white complex-
ion, pulling at him, making him hurt inside. He should
have taken better care of her; she had no one else but
him. "Here, give me Boyd's bloody mail and we'll
take you back—"

"No." She clutched the mail to her chest, shaking
her head. "I'm not going to collapse under the weight
of a few pieces of mail. I'm not an invalid. Please
don't treat me like one. I just want to lie down for a
while."

Gabe held up his hands, surrendering. "Fine. Don't
get all worked up, I'm just trying to look after you. Do
you have any objection to my walking back to the
house with you, or is that an insult to your indepen-
dence as well?"

"It's your house." Her voice sounded small and
defeated.

"I really wish Doc Hornbaker would get here,"
Gabe muttered, staring at her intently. "I'd feel better if he had another look at you. You're just not
yourself."

A.J. turned away before he could see the stinging
tears that threatened. *Not myself,* she thought through
the haze of bewildering images and feelings that tumbled through her mind with nauseating speed. *If only
that were true...*

Six

___

While A.J. slept the afternoon away, Gabe fretted ten years off his own life.

He paced back and forth on the front porch for nearly an hour, looking for signs of Doc Hornbaker, wondering what on earth was keeping him. He thought about driving into Ophir to get him, but he didn't want to leave A.J. alone. Neither did he think it wise to wake her up and take her into town with him. Each time he tiptoed to her room to check on her—which was on the average of every fifteen minutes—she was curled up on her side and sleeping like a baby. Obviously she needed rest. There was nothing he could do for her but to wait and be patient, and he'd never been good at either.

Finally he decided he would go crazy if he didn't find something useful to occupy his time. He considered going out behind the house and chopping some firewood but thought the noise might bother A.J. He thought about sharpening his fillet knife or waterproofing his new hiking boots or maybe tying a couple of new Olive Woolly Bugger flies, but none of those things really appealed to him.

So he went and picked some flowers.

He didn't have to go far. They grew in wild abundance in the woods behind the house—mountain daisies, sego lilies and bluebells. He arranged them in a mason jar—he didn't own anything as civilized as a glass vase—in what he thought was a very artistic fashion, with meadow grass as a filler. He tried the flower arrangement on the fireplace mantel, but it looked all wrong sitting there beside the dusty bourbon bottle. Instead, he decided to give it a home on the kitchen table, where it smelled very nice and would provide a centerpiece for dinner. A.J. would appreciate his wildflower bouquet, he was sure. And for reasons he really didn't care to look at too closely, he found great satisfaction in doing something for no other reason than to please A.J. It was uncharacteristic and sentimental, and it made him feel quite proud of himself. He couldn't remember the last time he'd been proud of himself. It was a good feeling.

He found a Scrabble game in the closet and set it out on the coffee table. After dinner, A.J. might enjoy sitting in front of the fire and playing a quiet game of Scrabble. That wouldn't be too tiring for A.J., and he liked the idea of looking across the table at her, laughing with her, helping her to relax. Almost as if they were... a couple. As if she belonged here where he could care for her. She had no one else in the world, he told himself over and over. Only him to depend on, to make her comfortable and safe. And now that he was becoming accustomed to having someone besides himself to think about, he didn't mind it at all.

She needed him. She was vulnerable and helpless and dependent on him, and no one knew how long her amnesia would last. As long as she needed him, he would be there for her. Today, tomorrow, the day after... as long as it took.

Doc Hornbaker finally arrived at sunset. He apologized for the lateness of the hour, explaining that he had had car trouble. He carried a bulging paper sack in one hand, his black medical bag in the other.

"Theo was going to come with me," he said, following Gabe into the kitchen. "Matter of fact, he was in the car with me when Roy Cobb stopped us right in the middle of the intersection. Someone had stuck a potato in the exhaust pipe of the mail truck, and he wanted to press charges. He didn't know who to charge, but he was damn well determined to make a federal case of it." He stopped abruptly, his eyes widening as he saw the colorful wildflower bouquet on the table. "Hells bells. What's that?"

Gabe colored furiously. "Well, what does it look like, Archie? It's a bunch of flowers."

"Hells bells," the stunned doctor said again. "I never expected to see such a thing on Gabe Coulter's kitchen table. Watch yourself, son. She's actually softening you up a little with her little feminine touches.''

"I picked them." Gabe's grudging voice was barely audible.

"What's that you say?"

Gabe glared a warning at him. "I picked the bloody flowers, all right? I *like* the bloody flowers! Is it such a big deal?"

Doc Hornbaker's lips twitched. "Not at all. Those are truly fine bloody flowers. Now may I see our patient?"

"She's taking a nap. She's been asleep for most of the afternoon. I'm worried about her, she didn't look well this afternoon."

"What about her memory? Any progress there?"

Gabe shrugged. "Not much. She remembered she liked French toast, and she had flashbacks of some school teacher she had when she was younger. That's about it."

"Actually, that's very encouraging. The rest will come in good time." Gabe set his paper sack down on the table. "Theo's wife put together a few things A.J. might need while she's here. To tell you the truth, I don't think you'll be inconvenienced too long. Her head injury wasn't all that serious, and she's a healthy young woman. Theo checked the missing persons reports, but nothing came up. He's going to contact the authorities in Denver, Cheyenne and Salt Lake and see if they know anything, but it will take some time. He'll let you know just as soon as he has any information that might help. Don't you worry, one way or another, we'll find our answers."

Gabe let out a relieved breath he hadn't been aware he was holding. For now at least, A.J. would be staying right here. "So what you're saying is, there's nothing we can do now but...wait?"

Archie took his sweet time answering. "That's about the size of it. Something tells me you're not finding this situation quite as unbearable as you thought you would."

"I'm not thrilled about it, but I'll see it through." Gabe avoided Archie's twinkling eyes, feeling the dull flush spread to his neck. He really disliked doctors at times. They thought they knew everything. "I'll let A.J. know you're here. There's a soda in the fridge if you'd like a drink."

"Oh, one more thing." Archie's deadpan voice caught Gabe in midretreat. "That's a fine tree house you made yourself outside, son. A damn fine tree house."

Without looking at him, Gabe lifted his hand high in the air, middle finger flying and marched out of the room.

The fire burned low on the hearth. The Scrabble game awaited. Archie Hornbaker was long gone, after giving A.J. a stern admonition to curtail any construction projects for the next day or two. She wasn't to overdo, she wasn't to climb trees and she wasn't to worry. Her memory had already started to return; it was just a matter of time before she would be back where she belonged. Just a matter of time.

Gabe was slumped on the sofa literally twiddling his thumbs while he waited for A.J. to sort through the clothes Archie had brought for her. She'd been gone forever. Well, not forever, but at least thirty minutes. It was amazing how empty the room seemed without her. She hadn't said much during dinner; Archie had done most of the talking, eyes twinkling in Gabe's direction while he reminisced about the magnificent split-level tree house with the genuine cedar-shake roof he and his younger brother had built some sixty years ago. It still stood, by George, a monument to Hornbaker ingenuity and craftsmanship. He'd be happy to give Gabe a few tips on reinforcing and waterproofing if Gabe asked nicely.

Gabe had been too worried about A.J. to pay much attention to Archie's not-so-subtle teasing. Something was wrong. She was too quiet, she avoided his eyes, she ate practically nothing. He didn't think she could be tired, since she'd slept most of the afternoon. Archie had pronounced her in good health. Frowning at the dying fire, Gabe replayed the day's events in his mind, wondering if he'd said or done something insensitive. He'd been a monumentally selfish person before moving to Ophir; after two years of thinking only of himself, it was likely he had become thoroughly obnoxious. He wondered if he should offer some kind of all-purpose apology, something like, "I realize I'm not the easiest person to be with. You've done a remarkable job of putting up with me." Maybe that would bring the smile back to her face. He missed her smile.

But when A.J. came back into the room, the smile was back. Slightly lopsided, but back all the same.

She paraded slowly past him, nose in the air, hands on her hips. "And next," she announced in a haughty voice, "we have the young amnesiac from parts unknown, modeling a striking polyester afternoon dress designed to complement the queen-size figure."

Gabe stared at the voluminous dress she wore, his jaw hanging slack. Enormous orange cabbage roses exploded on the shiny yellow fabric. The rounded neckline would have been modest on a three-hundred-pound woman; on A.J., it dropped completely off one shoulder, exposing her bra strap. The voluminous, ankle-length skirt wasn't quite long enough to hide a pair of orange patent leather platform heels. "You look like you're swimming in that dress," he said, a peculiar quiver in his voice.

She lifted an indignant eyebrow. "*Mr. Coulter.* I spend all this time trying to make myself look attractive and that's the best you can come up with?"

He nodded.

A.J.'s mouth twitched; then, with a spurt of laughter, she doubled over and buried her face in her hands. She was laughing too hard to talk clearly, her shoulders heaving with the rhythm of her chest. "You've...you've g-got to see the rest of these clothes. Theo's w-wife...is she...is she—" a gasp for air here "—a stout woman?"

"That's one way of putting it," Gabe said, fighting to breathe through his own laughter. "Juliette, Theo's wife, is very...healthy." He dropped his head back against the sofa, holding his arms over his aching sides. "I've never seen anything like that dress."

"It was very nice of her to think of me." Eyes streaming tears, A.J. dropped down beside Gabe on the couch, the dress billowing up around her slight body. "I really appreciate it, I do. Oh, this hurts. I can't stop. You should see the bathrobe she sent. I'd put it on for you, but you wouldn't be able to find me in it. Oh, I'm terrible. I'm sorry. I don't know why this seems so *funny*."

"Probably because you look so funny." He reached out and knuckle-rubbed the top of her head, loving the way her bangs tangled with her wet lashes. She looked like a six-year-old playing dress-up in her mommy's clothes. "You'd do better borrowing my clothes while you're here."

Trying to control herself, A.J. nodded and giggled and hiccuped, all at once. "You think?"

"I think." He looked at her sitting there next to him and thought he had never seen anything so beautiful. His smile remained, cutting deep in his cheeks, but the look in his eyes softened to curiosity. Such a hold she had on him, and after so short a time. She smiled, and his heart twisted in every direction. She cried and he ached. They laughed together, and the laughter came from somewhere new inside his soul, somewhere fresh and still innocent.

You would be so easy to love.

The thought came unbidden. He stared at her, feeling his heart begin to softly pound. "Damn," he whispered, his lips barely moving.

"What?" She tipped her head sideways. "What's wrong?"

So young. She looked so young with her ruffled hair and the hectic flush of emotion in her smooth cheeks. He swallowed hard, wondering where the hell his common sense had gone. "I just realized . . ."

She waited, her smile uncertain. "You just realized what?"

He looked in her eyes and gave it to her straight. "How hard it's going to be for me to let you go."

She stared at him in silence. A long moment went by, the fire making tired popping noises somewhere in the background. She moistened her lips, her small hands buried in the folds of her dress. "I'm here now," she whispered.

Gabe was utterly still. He held her dark, unblinking gaze, his throat so dry he couldn't even swallow. He knew he was crazy if he so much as touched her. The way he was feeling now, he would never be able to get through this without hurting them both. She had no idea what she was getting herself into, he was sure.

When he spoke, his voice was almost tortured. "I think you should go to bed. Now."

She shook her head . . . *no.* "You're always telling me to go to bed."

Gabe's chest was feeling painfully tight, as though a heart attack were imminent. "A.J., don't depend on me to take care of you tonight. I don't think I can."

"I don't want you to."

Her voice was low, husky, and it made the skin prickle on the back of his neck. She never looked away from him, not once. One of them was losing his or her mind; Gabe wasn't sure who. He looked at her bare shoulder, so sweet and fragile in the flickering light. She was lost in that idiotic dress....

He sucked in a hard breath as she placed her palms flat on his chest. Her brow was furrowed with concentration, as if touching him were the most important thing she had ever done.

"I can feel your heart," she said softly. "It's going so fast."

It was, thundering like a jackrabbit's. He had no control over his heart, or his hands, either. They went to her hair, her beautiful hair tinted red-gold by the firelight. He smoothed it away from her face, his fingers trembling. He could hardly believe how cool and silky it felt beneath his callused palms. His eyelids drifted closed as he memorized the sensation. A woman's hair. There was nothing softer, nothing finer in all the world. He wanted to bury himself in her hair.

"Please look at me," A.J. said. Nerves were in her voice, but there was also a determination that made his heart sink. He couldn't fight them both.

Their eyes met. Gabe tried to think of tomorrow, when the light of day would bring a sobering reality, but he couldn't concentrate. So many things were pulling at him—the rise and fall of her breathing, the way her lips parted ever so slightly, the warm pressure of her hands on his shirt. Drawing him in.

"You're scaring me to death," he said tightly.

"Gabe," she said softly.

His name, on her lips for the first time. The last of his resolve crumbled. His palms moved to frame her face as he slowly closed the distance between them. His mouth touched hers tentatively, the long-awaited kiss as light and fragile as a whisper. There was an exquisite eroticism in the restraint of the embrace, the quiet of the room, the brand-new door that was slowly opening. Her mouth parted on a sigh of pure, sweet pleasure, then opened wider as his tongue touched inside. A low groan came from deep in Gabe's throat and his heart beat harder. He hadn't expected this swell of feeling. This wondering pleasure was all new to him, leaving him tingling and trembling.

He lifted his head, wondering if he looked as stunned as he felt. He saw it in her eyes, as well—the awareness that something more was happening here than just a kiss.

"I'm shaking," he whispered.

She lifted her hand for him to see. "I'm shaking, too."

"This has to stop now...." But his eyes were half-closed before his mouth took hers again, this time without reserve. What had begun as a tentative stirring suddenly took hold of them, obliterating thought and conscience. The kiss was wide and deep and lush, pulling their bodies together in a cocoon of heat. Her hands went to his neck, clinging there, tangling helplessly in his long, thick hair. His arms closed around her small, slight body, dragging her tightly against him. He could feel her breasts crushed against his chest, smell the old-fashioned scent of lavender from the fabric of her dress. His body grew thick and hard almost instantly. In some distant part of his brain he truly wanted to stop, knowing the lasting hurt this could cause them both. But it was so hard, so hard when he was body to body with her at last. He'd been so lonely, long before he had hidden himself away in this isolated country. He was tired of pretending he needed no one and nothing.

They went on kissing and kissing with frantic, sucking noises, trembling sighs and wandering hands. When at last he pulled back, his blue eyes were fever-bright and his shirt was undone halfway down his chest. A.J.'s lips were shining wet and her breathing came quick and hard. Her dress was twisted side-ways, riding high on her hips and revealing the bur-geoning curve of one breast. That damned dress.

They looked deep into each other's eyes for a strained moment, neither of them daring to move. Then, biting down on his lip, he lifted his hands to her breasts. He watched her eyelids close as his fingers cupped and kneaded the tender mounds, heard the groan of astonishment deep in her throat. He pushed down the lacy edge of her bra, deciding not to damn her dress after all. Her nipple was warm and erect, the color of roses.

"You're beautiful," he said hoarsely, dipping his forehead against hers as he continued to stroke and fondle. "So perfect, so sweet . . ."

"I feel . . . sweet." She shivered, warm and sensu-ous against him. "Like a peach, juicy and hot from the sun . . . delicious . . ."

He groaned against her neck, his tongue tasting her skin. "You're making this so hard. It's not right—"

"It feels right." Her voice was wistful and dreamy. "It feels so right. . . ."

He swallowed convulsively as she arched and yearned against him, her swollen breasts filling his palms. Her hands were splayed over his bare chest, trembling and slightly damp. Gabe felt as if he were drifting somewhere above the scene, watching a ritual as old as time unfolding in thick slow motion. He saw her tousled hair bathed in fire colors, saw the way her head fell back, the way their bodies twisted into each other. Sexuality shimmered between them, dark and magical. They touched with tongues and lips and shaking hands, slowly freeing themselves from the bonds of self-consciousness and hesitation. Time stopped, pooling in the corners of the shadowed room. What Gabe was learning about this woman involved all his senses, all his concentration. Nothing was more important than the shape of her lips, the fragrance of her skin, the sweet caress of her hands on his face. It was all he could do to stop himself from pressing her backward onto the couch and taking her that last, irrevocable step. But he couldn't. The possibility of hurting her was far more painful than denying himself.

And so A.J.'s damned, damned dress stayed right where it was, falling off one shoulder, her bare breast gleaming like ivory in the flickering light. Her nipple was wet and hard from his hungry kisses, her nails were cutting into his shoulders and sweat was breaking out on Gabe's brow, but still he held back. For the first time in his life, it was more important to him to be noble than victorious. When her asking fingers went beneath his shirt to the waistband of his jeans, he stopped her with his hand, biting his lip to keep from swearing out loud.

"W-what?" A.J. was gasping, her face buried against his throat. "Gabe—"

He spoke through clenched teeth. "That's it. Either I'm going for a walk or you're going to bed. One of us is out of here, *now.*"

"What's wrong?" She pulled back, looking at him with passion-drenched eyes. "What did I do? I thought you wanted—"

"I do. No, I don't. Damn it." Gabe was learning more about frustration than he had ever thought possible. No wonder there were so few heroes in the world. "Not like this. You're alone, you're vulnerable, you could wake up in the morning and remember there's someone else—"

"There's no one else." The words were out before she could catch herself.

"A.J., you don't know that." He replaced the flimsy cup of her bra and arranged the neckline of her dress with all the finesse of a hot-and-bothered sixteen-year-old. "You don't know anything. Literally. Damn it. How did I get myself into this? I swear that's going to be my epitaph—'How did I get myself into this?' It fits me perfectly."

A.J. swallowed painfully. She could see the splotches of heat on his face, feel the sexual tension emanating from his body. This wasn't fair to him. She knew she should tell him the truth. That there was no need to protect her, that Angel Conaught was more than capable of looking out for number one.

But she couldn't.

She rose on shaky knees. "Maybe you're right. I should go to bed."

He slumped back on the couch, staring at her with brooding eyes. His shirt was open nearly to the waist, exposing the taut, inviting muscles of his neck and chest. "There's no maybe about it. I'm not exactly famous for my selfless nature."

"Maybe I'm not worth it," A.J. whispered. "Have you thought of that?"

His faint smile was disbelieving. "Not once. Some people in this world—not many, but some—deserve to be protected from reality as much as possible. You're one of them, brown eyes."

"Gabe—"

"Call me Mr. Coulter." Wry amusement mingled with the strain in his voice. "At least tonight. It might help me remember my responsibilities."

She bowed her head before he could see the misty tears in her eyes. His genuine concern tore at her heart. For the first time in her life, someone was caring for the billion-dollar baby with no ulterior motive. She couldn't give that up by telling him the truth—yet. She wanted to be A.J. as long as she could. She only wished Gabe Coulter could protect her from reality forever.

She wrapped her arms around her waist, squeezing the sides of her aching, swollen breasts. "You make me happy." Her voice was thick and husky and strange. "I've never been . . ."

But she couldn't finish the thought, and there was nothing she could do but press her lips together and leave the room.

* * *

She flopped down onto her bed, trying to ignore the yearning aftershocks shimmying downward through her body. The sound of the front door opening and closing told her that Gabe was having his own problems relaxing. She wanted to go after him so badly she rolled onto her stomach and pounded a pillow with her fists.

Without a doubt, the man could kiss. The aching loneliness that had taken Angel Conaught from one romantic entanglement to another had seldom resulted in physical expression. There was just no getting around it—a sexual relationship involved a certain amount of trust, and trust was a rare and precious commodity. She knew what it was to long for a spiritual connection with another human being, but her body had never experienced this intense, aching need to be filled. This was terrible. It was horrible.

She wanted more.

Lying in the darkness, she squeezed the wadded material of her dress between her legs and tried to understand what was happening to her. Emotions she had never realized she was capable of were coming alive inside of her. Her memory might have returned, but she was still a stranger to herself. In a curious way it was a relief. Honesty compelled her to admit there had never been a great deal to admire in the spoiled, insecure socialite named Angel Conaught. She'd been prone to thoughtlessness, recklessness and the occasional pique when life didn't go her way. But the woman called A.J. who paraded about in ill-fitting dresses and sketched blueprints of tree houses and adorned her hair with dental floss had real possibilities.

She sat up in the middle of the bed, twisting one long strand of hair around her finger and staring at nothing, remembering everything. Gabe's hands squeezing her tingling flesh, his tongue and teeth making her gasp and arch, his beautiful eyes growing drowsy with sexual heat. A strange euphoria came over her, making her shiver and bite down hard on her lip.

When she forgot her doubts and inhibitions, when she trusted without question, her sexuality took on a whole new dimension. The circumstances that had brought her together with Gabe had been nothing short of a miracle. Would it be such a terrible thing if she held on to that miracle a little longer? She couldn't bear the thought of going through the rest of her life asking herself what might have been.

She didn't know what was right or wrong. But for the first time in her life, she knew what she needed.

Seven

Went into Ophir to have a little talk with Theo. Be back in a couple of hours. Please don't play with the stove. Orange juice in the fridge, cereal in the cupboard.

Please don't play with the stove.

Mr. Coulter

Mr. Coulter.

A.J. reread the signature on the note, then dropped it onto the kitchen table with an unladylike snort. Not exactly a loving message. It had been very deflating to wake up this morning and find him gone. She didn't like it one bit, especially since she had spent the better part of the night twisting and turning in bed, anxious for the moment when the sun would finally rise and she could see him again. She'd shampooed her hair and dressed in a wraparound sundress that fit quite nicely, after she'd wrapped it around herself three times. The whole process had taken less then twenty minutes, a far cry from the hours and hours she used to spend in front of the mirror. Her priorities had done an unexpected about-face in the past three days.

She wasn't quite sure how to amuse herself while Gabe was gone. She knew the hot spots in Los Angeles and New York, she knew the most exclusive shops in London and the best restaurants in Paris, but she didn't know how to amuse herself in Ophir. Apparently playing with the stove was out. The only reading material Gabe had about the house dealt with things like trout physiology, wading techniques and nymph fishing, whatever that was. She wasn't too keen on taking a walk through a chipmunk-infested wilderness. Which left her all dressed up—or rather, wrapped up—with no place to go.

So she decided to snoop.

She had the best intentions. Gabe Coulter was a mystery to her—a vital, intelligent and sophisticated man who, at the ripe old age of forty, lived a life more isolated than Heidi of the Alps. She wanted to know more about him. She wanted to know everything.

She'd never been in his bedroom. She tiptoed down the hallway, looking over her shoulder now and then as if she expected him to jump out and catch her. His door was closed. She hesitated before it, chewing on one nail and asking herself if she was really the sort of person who would invade another's privacy. She decided the answer was yes, and slowly opened the door.

The room slept in shadows, curtains drawn over a hazy rectangle of daylight. Feeling like a burglar, she crossed to the rumpled bed. The pillow was on the floor, the sheets were hanging off one side, a patchwork quilt snarled into a knot at the foot of the mattress. He hadn't slept well, either, she thought with pure feminine satisfaction. As a matter of fact, it looked as if he hadn't slept at all. She appreciated his restraint, she did ... but sincerely hoped he'd learned his lesson. Time was so precious, and they had so much to discover about each other. With all her innocent hunger and youthful optimism, it never occurred to her that his caution might be justified.

She sat down gingerly on the edge of the bed, running her palm over the white cotton sheet. It was cool to the touch, but she imagined she could feel the heat from his body. She could see him, his body sprawled naked in the moonlight, long hair tumbled in wild shadows, tension and uncertainty tugging at his muscles, his mind full of *her*.

Oh, Mr. Coulter.

She was feeling a little hot. Fanning her flushed face with her hand, she looked elsewhere for distraction. Next to the reading lamp on the bedside table was a small tablet of graph paper. On the top page was a pencil drawing that looked something like a doghouse, although the scribbled lettering across the top said "wishing well." Plans for another project, she realized with a smile. His artwork was absolutely terrible. She laughed out loud as she read the circled note at the bottom of the paper: Change pitch on roof. Looks like a damn doghouse.

She was relaxing a little now, feeling more like she was just visiting his room instead of intruding. She wandered about, parting the curtains and looking at the view from his window, setting a wooden rocking chair in motion with her hand, wondering why it rocked sort of diagonally instead of straight back and forth. She opened his closet door and counted the dress shirts—none—and the denim and plaid work shirts—nine. No suits. No ties. Not one single pair of shiny shoes, unless you counted the rubber galoshes.

Everything made her smile. She'd never met a man like Gabe Coulter in her life. He had an old-fashioned manner about him that she found incredibly touching. And he seemed to need so little to make him happy. That in itself was absolutely amazing to one who had been raised with all the privileges and possessions of royalty, yet never felt content. She thought of the way Gabe whistled beneath his breath when he set a fire in the fireplace, the way he closed his eyes and savored the aroma of his coffee before he drank. And she recalled the soft pleasure in his eyes when he looked at her, as if seeing something rare and precious she'd never seen in herself. . . .

Her thoughts came to an abrupt halt as she heard a hammering on the door. She jumped sky-high, half expecting Gabe to barrel into his bedroom any second and catch her red-handed. Then logic caught up with her and she realized he would hardly announce his arrival by knocking on his own front door. Cheeks flushing guiltily, she practically ran to the front room, then stopped, took a deep breath and put her ear to the door, listening. After all, she was alone in the wilderness. Who was to say what sort of strange, uncivilized type of—

"Hello, it's Boyd Berrenger!" The former meteorologist had a deep, booming voice that carried very well. "Anyone home? I have news, people. Hey, it's going to rain out here! Hellooo?"

A.J. opened the door, a cool wind blowing straight at her face. "Hello, Boyd. Gabe's not here right now. He went into Gopher."

"You won't believe this!" Without invitation he strode into the room, his long khaki coat flying open behind. "It came to me out of the blue late last night, and I almost hightailed it straight over here, except there was no moon and I'm not really wonderful with directions in the dark, and I didn't want to fall into the reservoir. Anyway, I remembered where I'd seen you before." He turned with a flourish in the middle of the room to make his announcement, feet planted wide apart. "I don't know why it didn't come to me sooner. I've seen you often enough. The amazing thing is..." he paused, giving her an arrested look. "What's that you say? Gabe went hunting gophers?"

"I meant Ophir." A.J. closed the door, walked slowly to the sofa and sat down, her head bent so that her hair fell over her face. "Gabe drove into Ophir to talk to Theo."

"Well, who needs Theo when you have Boyd Berrenger? I've solved your mystery. I know who you are, and I can hardly *believe* it!" When there was no immediate response from A.J., he repeated loudly, "Did you hear me? I know who you are. You're saved! You're found!''

I'm lost, A.J. thought, looking up at him with woeful eyes.

Her subdued reaction seemed to take the wind out of Boyd's sails. He looked at her quizzically, his head cocked back on his long, thin neck. "Hells bells," he said finally. "I get it. You already remembered, didn't you? And here I thought I was going to be hailed as the heroic meteorologist. You know, I'm really surprised it didn't come to me the first second I saw you. I've seen your picture dozens of times. Just a few months ago you were on the front pages of all the tabloids when your..." He winced then, realizing what he had been about to say. "Oh, boy. I didn't mean to remind you of...oh, boy."

"It's all right." A.J.'s bare toes curled on the cold plank floor. "You can say it. When my father died. I remember everything, Boyd. My father's heart attack, the reporters and photographers at the funeral...I remember it all."

Boyd swallowed audibly, shifting his weight from one foot to the other. Finally he sat down beside her on the sofa and folded his arms. "I don't know about you," he muttered, "but this is just about the damnedest conversation I've ever had. I have no idea what to say next. I don't even know what to call you. Angel's a very nice name, but...you seem more like an A.J., you know?"

"I know." She smiled faintly. "When I was at boarding school in Switzerland, most of my friends called me A.J. No wonder it felt so natural when Gabe christened me.''

"Boarding school in Switzerland." Boyd shook his head, whistling softly. "None of my friends went to boarding school in Switzerland. Max Crocker lived with his aunt while he went down to Phoenix Tech, but—well, that's neither here nor there, is it? I'm babbling. I don't often talk to famous people. Well, once I got to interview Willard Scott via satellite, but he was sort of a soul mate, so I did okay.'' He was running out of air, but not completely. "You're engaged to Corwin Slade, aren't you? The guitar player? I remember reading about it.''

A.J.'s lips tightened. "I was. We broke it off a few weeks ago.''

"I remember hearing something about a baseball player.…''

"Football player," she said dully. "Donny Racine. We were engaged last year, but it didn't work out.''

"I see." Boyd's stupefied tone made it obvious he didn't see at all. "Well, you must keep very busy.''

A.J. smiled bleakly. "Oh, I do. Getting engaged and unengaged is very time-consuming. Not too productive, though, especially with the sort of men I manage to find.''

Boyd was too confused to be tactful. "Then why on earth—''

A.J. squirmed on the couch. "I suppose if I was honest with myself, I'd admit I simply wanted attention. Not just anyone's attention—my father's. My mother died when I was born and my father never did really warm up to me. He was a very powerful man who was completely dedicated to protecting the fortune he'd acquired. The only time he gave me his undivided attention was when I was irritating him. So...I irritated him as often as possible." She closed her eyes, understanding her past actions with more clarity than she might have wished for. "Not a very original story, is it? One impossible devil child, five impossible fiancés in three years and too many regrets to count."

Boyd didn't say anything for a moment. Then, hesitantly, he said, "It sounds pretty original to me. Personally, I don't know a single soul who has had five..." He stopped, thinking better of that particular remark. "You know what I don't understand? When Gabe found you down by Cottonwood Creek, what in the world had happened? Why was someone like you wandering around alone in the middle of the Sawatch Mountains?"

A.J. hung her head, tugging on her bangs. "It's not such a mystery, considering my track record. After my father died, I realized my relationship with Corwin was as misguided as everything else I'd ever done. I broke off our engagement and flew to Denver to stay with some friends. Corwin followed me, determined to change my mind. I'd never seen him like that. He wasn't just losing a fiancée, he was losing all the money she had inherited. Anyway, we had a terrible fight, and things got really nasty. I borrowed my friend's car and left in the middle of the night. I had no idea where I was going, I just wanted to get away from everything. Did I tell you I don't have a driver's license?"

Boyd reared back his head. "Hells bells. It isn't because you're underage, is it?"

She smiled crookedly. "I'm twenty-four years old, Boyd. I just never got around to getting a license. I really don't know how I ended up in the mountains. When the sun came up there were all these trees and hills and a narrow strip of asphalt that was more like a roller coaster than a road. I lost control of the car—it was a miracle it didn't happen sooner—and ran it down a fairly steep ravine. I remember hitting my head, then . . . nothing. The next thing I knew, I was waking up under a picnic table with vampire chipmunks all over me. I suppose when I regained consciousness, I tried to go for help, but I'm not sure how I—"

And at that point the front door swung open and A.J.'s heart completely stopped beating. Gabe, came in, dressed in boots and jeans and zipped into a soft suede jacket. Behind him, the doorway was filled with a bubbling, steel gray sky and wind-whipped leaves. His long hair blew forward, over his collar and cheeks. He stared at the unlikely duo on the sofa over a bulging grocery bag he held in one arm. A muscle jumped in his jaw, visible from clear across the room. "If you climbed through one of my windows again," he told Boyd flatly, "if you scared A.J. even the slightest bit, if you even *thought* about doing any more of that silent tracking, I swear I will—"

"This is not a day for threats," Boyd replied, shaking his finger at Gabe. "We should all be celebrating. I can't tell you how relieved I am that..." He broke off abruptly, staring down at A.J.'s fingers which were

suddenly clamped like a vise grip on his arm. "Ouch,"
he said.

A.J. jumped right in with brittle cheerfulness.
"Boyd just dropped by to see how everything was. It's
been nice to have company while you were out."

The wind pushed the open door into the back of
Gabe's boot; he kicked it closed, frowning at Boyd.
"As usual, you've lost me, Boyd. Why should we be
celebrating? And why are you so relieved, or dare I
ask?"

Boyd's startled gaze lifted to A.J.'s. He cleared his
throat once, then again before answering. "I am incredibly relieved that you're home safely," he told
Gabe. "Nasty storm brewing out there. Low pressure
moving in, sixty percent chance of thundershowers. I
should be heading home to the old Winnebago right
away. My moccasins are very comfortable, but they're
not waterproof. You'll just have to celebrate without
me."

"Celebrate *what?*" Gabe demanded.

"Oh, well…we're just so darn happy you're home.
It's pleasant for everyone." Choking a little, Boyd rose
to his feet. He was flustered; he'd never been good at
improvisation. As a weatherman, he'd always relied
heavily on TelePrompTer screens. "I have to go now.
Right away. I've enjoyed talking to you, A.J. We'll
have to continue this conversation very soon."

"Let me walk you outside, Boyd." A.J. scrambled
off the sofa, deep color stealing up to the roots of her
hair. "Some fresh air will do me good. Gabe, I'll just
walk Boyd outside."

"So you said." Gabe stepped to one side, so as not to be trampled by the sudden exodus from his living room. The wind and the smell of rain flew in, A.J. and Boyd rushed out.

After a thoughtful moment, Gabe walked to the kitchen with his groceries. He would put the ice cream in the freezer and the milk in the fridge...and then the nervous amnesiac with the bare toes and the pathetically guilty expression was going to do a little explaining.

"Just what the heck do you think you're doing?" Boyd groused. He was stomping back and forth on the front porch, waving his long arms wildly in the wind. "Gabe doesn't know, does he? He has no idea you've gotten your memory back! Do you realize what an idiot I looked like in there?"

"Yes," A.J. said.

"I'll tell you, for two cents, I'd—" The meat of Boyd's threat was lost in a roll of thunder overhead— "...and why shouldn't I? Why the heck shouldn't I?"

"Boyd, listen to me." A.J. wasn't dressed for a mountain storm; her bare arms were chicken-skinned and her teeth were chattering. "I know this all seems c-crazy to you, but I need a little more time. I'm going to tell Gabe everything, but...not just yet."

"Why not? Why keep it from him? I can't think of a single reason why Angel Conaught would want to stay in a place like *Ophir* with a man she barely—" Abruptly he stopped talking and moving. He stared at A.J. through a curtain of wind-tossed hair. "Maybe I can think of one reason. Are you and Gabe...?"

"It's not like that." She hugged herself tightly, standing on one leg while she rubbed the sole of one cold foot on the top of her other cold foot. "I mean, it could be, but... there's more to it than that. In the past few days, even with everything that's happened to me, I think I've been—" funny how hard it was to put it in to words —"I think I've been happy. There are no expectations here for me to live up—or down—to. I haven't worried about my clothes or my hair or my makeup. I haven't seen a reporter or heard a telephone or looked twice in a mirror. Gabe's seen me looking like the wrath of God, he's let me use his hairbrush and wear his clothes and talk him into building the most terrific tree house—"

"I noticed that," Boyd replied, momentarily distracted. "It looks like a very sturdy structure. You know, if there were to be a flash flood, that would be a perfect place to... no, we can't get off the subject. A.J., what about your friends, your family? It's not fair to let them think you've just vanished off the face of the earth. They'll be going crazy worrying about you."

"No, they won't." A.J. shook her head, shivering to her toes. "The closest family I have is a great-aunt who lives in London. And it will never occur to my friends to worry about me, either. They're accustomed to my disappearing on a whim. Boyd, I can't tell you how important this is to me. I want a little more time to see myself through Gabe Coulter's eyes. It's not as selfish as it sounds, either. I think I make him happy. Last night I actually made him *laugh*."

Boyd's eyes stretched. "No way. Out loud?"

"So hard he got tears in his eyes. So maybe having me here isn't such a bad thing for either of us. Maybe it was meant to be."

"This is mind-boggling." Boyd leaned over the porch railing and plucked at his beard. "First, you can't remember and it scares you to death, then you do remember and want to forget. What a trip. All right, I guess I'll just have to believe you know what you're doing." He glanced at her over his shoulder. "You do know what you're doing, don't you?"

"I think so." There was always a first time, A.J. reasoned.

"I wish you luck, then. I'd better take off before this storm gets any worse." He took the porch steps in one jump, yelping as his soft moccasins landed on a sharp-edged rock. "These shoes need soles—my poor feet are black and blue. How did the Indians take the pain?"

A.J.'s wind-chilled lips crooked in a stiff smile. "Bye, Boyd. Thank you for everything."

"I'll be in touch." He limped halfway across the yard, then turned and shouted, "You really made Gabe Coulter laugh?"

"Piece-a-cake."

He scratched his head and grinned. "Maybe you do know what you're doing."

Gabe's ulcer was on the warpath.

He took a hefty swig from the bottle of Maalox antacid he'd bought, then capped it and put it into the fridge. *Maalox,* he thought dejectedly. The first time in months he'd needed it, and why? The answer was very short; just two little letters short.

A.J.

His talk with Theo had been thoroughly frustrating. There were no leads on A.J., no missing person report that matched her description, no nothing. *All we can do is wait for something to turn up, Gabe.*

But Gabe wasn't sure just how long he could wait. Every man had his breaking point, and he was dangerously close to his. Which was why he had fought World War III in his bed all night long, thrashing around in a cold sweat, knowing if he went to her, she wouldn't turn him away. That was the hardest part. That was why he had raced off to find Theo this morning, hoping there would be some last minute development that would take it all out of his hands while there was still time.

And subconsciously praying there wouldn't be one.

He heard the front door close, the muscles in his neck and shoulders suddenly tensing, his ulcer whimpering. She came into the kitchen quietly, avoiding his eyes, checking the empty paper sack on the table to see if there were any groceries she could help put away.

"Boyd went home," she commented unnecessarily, folding the sack.

"Boyd should do that more often." Gabe had a few questions for her, but the faint blue cast of her lips distracted him. He realized for the first time she was dressed in some kind of a halter-top dress, which left her shoulders and arms exposed. Not to mention the fact that her feet were bare. "You're not dressed for the weather," he said abruptly. "When a storm hits up here, even in the summer, the temperature can drop twenty degrees in ten minutes. You should put on your sweats and some socks."

"I don't have any socks, and the sweat suit is in the washer. I did a load of laundry this morning. Don't worry—I didn't use any bleach, and I made sure to use cold water. I didn't want to ruin anything."

"Do I look worried? Anyone can manage a simple load of laundry." He didn't see the doubting face she pulled. He took the sack out of her hands and stuffed it into the drawer. "Come with me. I'll fix you up with something warmer to wear."

"Theo's wife sent a quilted robe I could put on over—"

"Then you have something to use for a blanket if you need it."

Biting her lip, A.J. trailed after Gabe into his bedroom, the very same room she'd made herself at home in just an hour before. Her heart kicked into a hectic beat as she wondered if she could have left something out of place. He would know she'd been snooping in his room, and he didn't seem to be in the best of moods.

"I've got a pair of long johns in here that ought to do the trick." Gabe went to his closet, reaching up to the top shelf where he kept his winter clothing. It wasn't by accident that he was providing her with the most shapeless, unappealing garment in the history of the world. "Here you go. Built-in tootsie warmers, and a nifty rear end escape hatch with buttons. You'll be warm as toast."

"Warm as toast," A.J. echoed tonelessly, holding the heavy cotton underwear with two fingers. This was a challenge for a woman who attended the spring fashion shows in Paris every year. Cabbage roses she could handle. Sweat suits were no problem. But did she honestly want this man to see her in bright red long johns that looked like something out of Li'l Abner? "I don't think they'll fit."

Gabe smiled grimly. "They don't need to fit. They just need to keep you warm."

Men. "Just the same, I think I'll put the sweats in the dryer and—"

"And you'll be a little blond ice cube by the time they're dry. Listen, A.J. Hear the rain on the roof? Hear the wind?"

She listened. It sounded as if three hundred chipmunks were tapping on the copper roof with itty-bitty hammers. Wind rattled the glass pane in the window. "It's getting bad out there," she admitted grudgingly.

"That's right. But we're lucky." His voice took on an irritating, singsong quality. "Do you know why we're lucky? Because we can put on a nice pot of stew and build a roaring fire and climb into a thick pair of good old long johns."

"Except that *we're* not climbing into the good old long johns, are we?" she muttered. "I'm the one who gets to do that."

But what I'd give to climb in there with you. Something changed in Gabe's face. He stared down at the floor, silently counting to ten, twenty...

"Your lips are moving," A.J. said curiously. "Gabe? What on earth are you doing?"

His eyes were fever-bright as he looked up at her. "Losing...my...mind," he said succinctly. "And call me Mr. Coulter, damn it." Before she could react, he turned away, pulling a white T-shirt from the dresser drawer and tossing it at her. "There. If you're suddenly so fashion conscious, wear that over the underwear. The layered look is real popular in Ophir this year. After you've changed, maybe the two of us could have a little fireside chat."

"A fireside chat?" A.J. clutched the underwear and T-shirt to her bosom, the very picture of guilt. "You can't have a fireside chat in the middle of the afternoon."

"Why?"

"Because...because there's no fire to chat beside, that's why."

"Then I'll just have to get one going, won't I?"

"What do you want to chat about?"

"A.J., if I didn't know better, I'd swear you had a guilty conscience about something."

"Why would I have a guilty conscience?" Her squeaky little voice could have belonged to either Chip or Dale.

"You tell me." Gabe's lips thinned to a straight, tight line. "Could it have something to do with Boyd? The two of you were looking awfully cozy when I came home. Snuggled up together on the couch like a couple of teenagers." He paused, then added darkly, "Guilty teenagers."

"You can't mean . . . you couldn't possibly think Boyd and I were . . . were . . ." She sputtered for a moment, torn between relief, indignation and amusement. Amusement won out. She doubled over with a shout of laughter, burying her face in the good old long johns. "With Boyd," she gasped almost joyously. "With *Boyd?* You're amazing, Mr. Coulter. I can't stand this. You're jealous, you're jealous, you're jealous. . . ."

Gabe had heard enough from this impudent bit of a woman. He said a bad word that A.J. heard quite clearly even through the red underwear, said it again, kicked the doorframe and stomped out of the room.

He could hear her laughing all the way down the hall.

Eight

He was a pathetic shell of a man.

This is what Gabe Coulter told himself as he stoked a fire big enough to turn the living room into a sweltering furnace. He'd been reduced to petty jealousy. To adolescent cursing. To losing his temper and kicking doorframes. He could only be grateful A.J. hadn't seen the flying finger he'd thrown her way as he'd walked out of the bedroom. He'd have no dignity left at all then.

He had completely lost control. He couldn't anticipate what he was going to do or say or feel anymore. Cold, clear logic had walked out the door the day A.J. had walked in. A peculiar sound escaped him as he hunched there in front of the fire, a cross between a groan and an embarrassed laugh. What would he do next? Even more terrifying, what would *she* do next?

He looked into the flames but saw only her face. Painfully, his voice softer than a whisper, he said, "I love you."

The sound of footsteps brought him to his feet. A.J. walked stiffly into the living room, an eye-popping vision in red long johns and a baggy white T-shirt. The built-in tootsie warmers were twice as long as her feet, dragging across the floor. The rear end escape hatch sagged pitifully below the frayed hem of the T-shirt. Where the underwear didn't hang, it bagged, where it didn't bag, it drooped. Her breasts and hips had completely disappeared. She still had a head, neck and shoulders, but that was all. Everything else was completely shapeless.

A.J. stated her position before he could get a word out. "You put me in this thing, *Mr. Coulter.* You said it wasn't important that it fit, only that it keep me warm. In the spirit of practicality I'm wearing this...less than flattering outfit. However, if you dare smirk, if you crack the tiniest smile, if you make the faintest sound that even resembles a laugh, there will be hell to pay. Excuse my language, but I didn't want any misunderstandings. I'm feeling a little sensitive right now."

Mute with shock, Gabe nodded his head automatically. His eyes traveled up and down her nonexistent figure, growing wider, brighter, wider still. His chest ached in the center of his breastbone; he realized with something akin to fear that a laugh was fighting to get out. It wasn't a faint sound that *resembled* a laugh, either.

A.J.'s face took on the same rose hue as the long johns. Her eyes narrowed a warning. "Don't," she said softly.

He choked. He gasped. He tried, tried so hard to control himself, but there were too many emotions tearing at him right and left, wearing him down. Caution was an impossibility. The laughter just exploded, ringing out above the rattling doors and windows and the sound of a hard rain hitting the tin roof. He bent in the middle just as she had done earlier, holding his sides, shoulders heaving. His mind told him to get a grip before there was hell to pay, then he'd take one look at her face and lose it all over again. Feeling slightly deranged, he staggered to the sofa and fell down, his feet bouncing on the rag rug. She'd never forgive him. He didn't want to hurt her feelings; he was so sorry. And he knew he was going to be even sorrier.

"L-listen." He could hardly get the words out, running amok as he was. "Need you to listen. Want to tell you...I l-love..."

But A.J.—or rather, Angel Conaught—was a beginner when it came to patience, understanding and tolerance. She wasn't used to being a spectacle, and she wasn't accustomed to being laughed at. She didn't like it. Her fists tightened until her knuckles were almost transparent. Her eyes blazed with just a hint of the glorious temper tantrums she had thrown in the past. Her little heart pounded furiously, though it couldn't be detected beneath her saggy, baggy outfit.

In that instant she disliked him almost as much as she loved him. And since self-control wasn't really her strong suit, she didn't hesitate to put her feelings into precise words.

"Up yours, Mr. Coulter."

Then, with as much dignity as a woman wearing red underwear could summon, she hitched up her dangling stocking feet and padded furiously away.

She didn't come out of her room the rest of the day. Not once.

A repentant Gabe knocked on her door and offered to bring her a bowl of stew for dinner, but she declined in no uncertain terms. Later on he made a trip outside to the workshop just to walk past her window, but the lights were out. He stuck his nose against the rain-wet window, barely able to make out a glimpse of a hunched figure covered with a bedspread.

He wasn't really sure how everything had gone so wrong, but it made him feel better to blame it on Boyd. Damn that Boyd.

Coming back inside, he was soaked and shivering, his shirt plastered to his back, his wet hair sticking to his neck. He took a hot shower, turning the water off twice because he thought he'd heard A.J. knocking on the bathroom door. Both times it turned out to be nothing more than wishful thinking.

On the way back to his bedroom, a towel slung around his hips, he paused by her door. Minutes ticked by. He didn't know what he was waiting for. Finally he whispered her name, but there was no answer. He tried again, in his normal voice.

Not a word. She was a confounded stubborn woman.

Grinding his teeth, clenching his fists, willing the fire in his stomach to subside, he went to his own room. Another night alone. He feared the verbal, physical and emotional foreplay of the past few days had made his body permanently taut. He wasn't comfortable, he wasn't at peace and he wasn't sleepy. He didn't bother with the light in his bedroom. He simply let the towel drop to the floor, tossed all the covering off the bed save for a single sheet, and climbed in. Yes, he was naked, yes he was cold. Hopefully it would have the same effect as putting an ice pack on certain parts of his body.

It wasn't until he had pounded his pillow into submission, kicked the sheet free from the bottom of the bed and folded his arms beneath his wet head that he realized he wasn't alone in the room. The rocking chair he had built with his own two hands was rocking.

He sat up with a jerk, the loose top sheet billowing and settling low on his waist. There was no moon on this stormy night, no light at all in the pitch-dark room, but her golden hair had a glowing luminescence all its own.

"Hello," A.J. whispered, her voice coming low and soft through the shadows. "It's just me."

Just you, Gabe thought painfully. He couldn't move, not a muscle.

The rocker stopped creaking. "This is where my courage gives out," she said. "It's amazing I got this far."

The room settled into a soul-deep quiet, all but the sound of the rain and the wind. Gabe stared at her hair, softly shining through the darkness. His throat was so dry it hurt. This was exactly what he wanted, and this was exactly what he was so afraid of.

"If I asked you to go," he whispered finally, "would you?"

She didn't answer, but he could see her golden head shake from side to side.

"You don't know what you're doing." Truer words were never spoken. Gabe thought they deserved repeating. *"You don't know what you're doing."*

"That's nothing new." Then, in a more hopeful, if somewhat shaky voice, she added, "But at least I know what I want. That's a step in the right direction, don't you think?"

"I don't think," Gabe growled, low in his throat, "that's my problem. A.J., don't depend on me to—"

"I'm tired of hearing that." She stood up abruptly, the rocker skidding backward on the floor. "I don't *depend* on you. I need you."

A radiating warmth seemed to be throbbing inside his legs, his arms, his chest. The cotton sheet around his lower body felt like a wool blanket, weighing him down, hot and heavy. He wanted it off. Conversely, his hands clutched it higher around his middle. It wasn't too late to save her, not while there was still ten feet between them.

"You listen to me," he ordered through clenched teeth.

She waited.

"You damn well listen to me," he said again, louder, pounding one fist on the bed.

She didn't move. "I'm *listening.*"

Damn, damn, damn, damn. Gabe closed his eyes, dropping one leg over the edge of the bed, pushing his foot hard on the floor for some kind of balance. Sweet girl, he wanted to tell her, can't you see I want to do the right thing? Go away, go away.

But what he actually heard his voice saying was, "You're too far away."

He thought he heard the sudden intake of her breath. A flash of white lightning illuminated the awkward steps she took toward him. He saw she was wearing his old blue sweatshirt, and nothing else. Thunder roared and wind keened, like something out in the wild night was hurting.

"It wasn't nice to laugh at me." The words seem to float on the darkness, small and uncertain.

"No."

Another step toward him. He could see her fingers plucking at the stretched-out hem of the sweatshirt. "You shouldn't have."

"Never again," he promised.

"I don't believe you," she said. There was faint amusement in her voice now, along with the nerves. "Gabe?"

"What?" Now both feet were on the floor. He was tense, poised on the edge of the mattress, still breathing only because he consciously willed himself to.

"This isn't easy for me. Would you please...I need you to..."

Standing there in front of him, she seemed all of seventeen years old, with her speech faltering and her hair tangled around her face and her eyes shining wide and dark. There was a powerful constriction in his heart, a desperate need to care for her and soothe her and fulfill her. He stood up in thick slow motion, as if the shadows fought his every move, clutching a knot of sheet at his waist. "I know, honey," he whispered. "I know."

She sighed and smiled then, a smile he could see glimmering in her eyes before it spread to her lips. The softest, sweetest smile, a smile that could easily put a grown man on his knees. "Then do with me what you will, Mr. Coulter," she said simply.

It was so hard for him, reaching out after pushing her—and the rest of the world—away for so long. There was a tangible pain in his chest as he slowly opened his arms, the sheet puddling over his feet in a soundless rush of air. In that moment, he felt his age, he felt his youth, he felt hunger and uncertainty and masculine knowledge and power... he felt it all. He *felt*.

"Do with me what you will," he echoed quietly.

And then she came home into his arms as if she'd done it a hundred times before, putting her cheek over his heart and clasping her hands behind his satin-smooth back. They rocked together, eyes closed, the storm sounds ebbing and flowing over the small house. And for a time, holding each other was enough, holding each other was everything. There was no urgency now; what would happen would happen.

A.J. pulled back her head, searching his eyes, touching his face with her hands. "I'm still not close enough," she said dreamily. "I've got all these *clothes* on."

Gabe tenderly kissed her forehead, the corner of her eye. "One sweatshirt?"

"Is one sweatshirt too many, I think." She stepped back and held her arms up in the air. "Help me, Mr. Coulter."

Gabe swallowed painfully. "Mr. Coulter is having a heart attack."

But help her he did, with clumsy hands and trembling fingers, tugging the shirt up and over her head, then tossing it out of sight and out of mind. They came together again, but this time flesh touched flesh, stomach to stomach, breast to breast. A.J. made a sound of agonized pleasure deep in her throat, arching into the cradle of his hips as his hands rolled slowly down her back to cup her buttocks. She felt his arousal, she felt the turgid points of his nipples, she felt the silky-coarse hair of his chest. With her eyes half-closed and her mouth softly parted, she rubbed her breasts against him, relishing the feeling of sculpting herself to this man's body. Never in her life had she felt such an acute sensitivity to another human being. Low and deep, her body began to soften and weep with desire. *This is almost too much to bear,* she thought hazily. *I didn't know, I didn't know I could feel so much.*

And it was right. For the first time in her life, it was right.

Gabe lifted his head, gazing down at her. "Look at you," he whispered hoarsely. "Oh, look at you. You're so young, so beautiful. I'm afraid to touch you."

She threaded her fingers through the long hair on either side of his face. Her hips burned against the proof of his desire. "You're sort of touching me already, don't you think?"

"Sort of." His hands moved to her waist, circling there, the tips of his fingers meeting on either side. "So tiny everywhere," he murmured. Then he slid his palms up and over her rib cage, cupping and lifting the aching weight of her breasts. "No, not everywhere. In some places you're very... generous."

"Generous." A.J. rolled the word around her tongue like sugar candy. "I like that. I feel generous. I want to open myself up to you, to give and give and give..."

"Heart attack," Gabe groaned. He lowered his lips to her neck, tasting the satin curves, kissing his way to the delicate ridge of her collarbone. She seemed so fragile to him; his heart swelled with more compassion than he knew he was capable of. He didn't want to hurt her, he didn't want to frighten her, he wanted to give and give....

"I love you," he whispered with a frantic wonder. All the emotion in his soul, all the pleasure and pain he was feeling, rode on those three small words. He buried his face in the hollow of her throat, breathing hard and fast, afraid to believe this was real. He didn't deserve a chance like this. God only knew why he had been allowed to feel this new life in his heart. "I would never hurt you. Never."

"I know." Her head fell back weakly as she gave all her concentration to learning, to experiencing. She bit her lip hard between her teeth as his mouth moved lower, closing over the tip of her breast with a hunger she felt in her deepest, most womanly parts. His teeth gently bit and tugged, his lips and tongue suckled like a baby feeding until she had to press her lips together to keep from sobbing out loud. She was dimly aware of the subtle blooming of her inner flesh, an almost imperceptible, softly pulsating release of moisture. Her hands were clinging to his shoulders, the musky smell of their arousal coming up between their bodies. Her eyes drifted closed; she pretended she was blind, letting her other senses discover and memorize him. She trusted him with everything she had, and with that trust came a freedom to enjoy the dark magic they created together. Her hands slipped over beautiful muscles and flat planes, her fingers trailed erotically through moist, warm hollows. She couldn't speak, there were no words to convey everything she was feeling.

She was panting now, weak in the knees, making little whimpering sounds. His mouth stifled her with a fierce, desperate kiss that went deep and hard, tongues instinctively imitating the act of love. He found himself pressing against the softest, yielding part of her, into her. He realized he had to slow down or lose control altogether. He picked her up in his arms and they tumbled onto the bed, rolling over, pressing themselves tightly together this way and that. He was above her, his hair drifting about his face as he stared hard into her eyes; then she twisted feverishly and was straddling his legs, kissing his nose and his chin and tongue-stroking his shining lips. Somewhere in the universe it was raining, somewhere the thunder rolled over mountaintops and lightning repeatedly cracked the sky. But here in Gabe's darkened room there was a different, quieter, more dangerous storm. Through it all, the realization wrung his heart. *You're here with me. This is really happening to us.*

He tried to be gentle, but there came a point when emotions shattered into a driving, overwhelming greed. He had a fierce need to touch and taste her everywhere, her belly, her back, between her thighs. Then she was lying on her back in the middle of the big bed, her legs parting, her fingers holding his shoulders to steady herself. She gave him total submission; it was there shining in her eyes when he poised himself above her. *Do with me what you will.*

For that instant, Gabe felt as though he were finally in perfect balance, a beautiful stillness spreading through the center of his being. His hands found her hips, lifting them toward him while he held her eyes. His hardness brushed across the place of damp, hot need, once, then again, probing slightly but never entering. The muscles in his arms and shoulders pulsated with tension, yet still he held back. With every stroke that promised fulfillment, she gasped slurred, half-formed sentences: "Oh, please...this feels so...I need . . . you feel so good . . . don't stop. . . ."

And then he was inside her, burying himself deep with a single stroke that nearly made him explode with pleasure. At last he had claimed the blood center of her, this mysterious, unknown woman who gave of herself so graciously. She sucked in her breath as he began to move within her. So little time they had had together, yet so much feeling and solace and love had come from it. Bound at last, an unlikely pair in this unexpected time and place.

A miracle, Gabe thought hazily, staring down at the golden head on his pillow. A woman beautiful enough for tears, sharing his bed, filling the empty places in his heart. How many times he had dreamed of this, of someone to hold and whisper to in the dark? He felt like a drowning man who had been pulled free of the water and flung up onto solid ground.

He wanted to make it gentle and lasting, but he had been too long without, too long alone. The rhythm changed as the fire swept through his body, becoming a frenzied dance he was powerless to control or contain. He was so afraid of hurting her, she was so small and tight and delicate. But surprisingly she was the one who pushed him over the edge, who thrust her hips against his with a desperate demand. It was amazing to him, to know her hunger was equal to his own. To know that she wanted him like that, buried inside of her, needing him as badly as he needed her. Saving his life.

There was a sudden, breathless pause in their joined movements, then he made an aching sound between a groan and a sob while his body plunged one more time, deep and hard. The pressure exploded in shock waves through his back, his shoulders and thighs as he felt himself spill into her. The pleasure was excruciat-

ing. He was reborn, naked and joyful and new. His
eyes widened, locking with hers in wonder and disbelief. He wanted to tell her what he felt, but there was
a burning knot in his throat, blocking whatever inad-
equate words he could have found. For one embarrassed, astonishing moment he thought he would cry.

When he could think and speak again, he touched
her face with a badly shaking hand and whispered,
"Forgive me. I meant to wait until you . . ."

"I didn't know . . . I was supposed to be first." Her
eyes danced for him even as she arched toward the
heavy fullness still inside her. She was all electric energy, pulsating, radiating inward. And Gabe knew. He
knew everything she needed, and he joyfully per-
formed the sensual magic that made her wet, hot and
nearly oblivious. In a slow, husky parody of polite
conversation, she added, "Anyway, it's going to be my
turn now."

And it was.

It was.

She was sleeping as soundly as a child when Gabe
came drifting back to the world of tumbled covers and
storm-shrouded darkness. They were facing one another, her legs tangled bewitchingly around his. He
could see the shape of her adorable nose, feel the cool
silk of her hair beneath his cheek. Her breathing was
deep and utterly peaceful, whispering like little kisses
over his lips. And somewhere beneath the rumpled
sheet, her small hand was curled confidingly into his.

At a moment like this, I could almost believe it's
forever. I'll be lying beside her every night for the rest

of my life. I'll be pulling back the covers when she hogs the bed...the way she's doing now. Some mornings I'll be sneaking off to make her breakfast in bed...French toast. And then we'll walk together outside, and I'll show her all my favorite places to go. I'll show her the wildflowers in the spring and the rusty, rainbow colors of the mountains in autumn. She'll scold me for leaving gobs of toothpaste in the sink. I'll have to break all the bad habits I've gotten into since I came here. And I'll have to fix the kitchen table so it doesn't rock. That's very important...

And she'll never leave me. She'll be my miracle forever.

Suddenly, as if she had heard his thoughts, she opened her eyes. For the longest time she stared at him, not speaking, not moving. Then she lifted her chin, kissing him solemnly on the tip of his nose.

"Good night, Mr. Coulter," she whispered.

He held her captive in a lazy, burning gaze, his thigh rubbing over hers beneath the sheet. "I wish you sweet dreams, love," he murmured in a gravelly voice. His hand went slowly wandering, over her rounded belly, down to the soft, swollen folds of her. "And just to make sure..."

Nine

Something was burning.

Gabe knew what it was before he opened his eyes. She'd beaten him out of bed. She was playing with the stove. And yes ... she had the radio turned on again. It sounded like polka music this time. How on earth had she found the radio? He'd hidden it in an empty cereal box in the cupboard.

Despite the threat of being blown to smithereens, he yawned and rolled his shoulders languorously and took a few moments to savor the memories of the night before. A smile came to his lips. She was here, she loved him, he loved her; the miracle lived on. Providing the stove didn't go boom.

He found a pair of jeans and pulled them on, then headed for the kitchen to rescue his ladylove from the big bad gas stove. As he had suspected, the makings of French toast were out on the counter. He could barely see the cast-iron griddle on the stove for all the smoke and fire that lapped around it.

"You might want to turn that down a bit," he suggested to the cook in a croaky, not-quite-awake voice.

She looked at him over her shoulder, giving him a wicked smile and a wiggle of her eyebrows. "If you can't stand the heat," she said, "get out of the kitchen. Good morning, Mr. Coulter."

He winced as he saw how close her flying hair came to the leaping flames. "Turn the gas down, honey. A low-flying plane might think we're signaling for help."

She made a face, but obediently turned the burner down. "I don't want sarcasm from you, Mr. Coulter. I want congratulations. I lit this stove with one single match. I was prepared to use a dozen or so, but I'm much better at the basics of country living than I realized. Nothing to it. We now have French toast up the yeeng-yang."

Gabe suppressed a smile, looking at a plate piled high with still smoking toast. "Don't we just."

"And I made juice. I noticed you don't drink orange juice, so I found some frozen grapefruit juice. I'm being so thoughtful this morning, don't you think?"

"More than you realize." His voice was dreamy and distracted; he was looking at the most wonderful view. The thoughtful cook wore a flannel shirt and a white dish cloth tied around her waist. The makeshift apron turned the shirt into a plaid miniskirt that barely covered her bottom. "Very, very thoughtful. Good morning."

She kept her back to him. "How are you feeling to-day?"

He kept his eyes on her back. "Oh, just fine. And you?"

"Quite well, thank you." There was a gurgle of laughter in her voice.

"A.J.?"

"Yes, Mr. Coulter?"

"Put down the spatula." He paused, then added politely. "Please, honey pie."

She balanced the spatula on the edge of the griddle, then slowly turned to face him, wiping her hands on the dish towel. "The spatula is down, snookums."

"I want to tell you..."

"You want to tell me...?" she prompted, smiling tentatively.

Their eyes locked, narrowed against the watery sun that lightened the walls of the room. He tried to tell her silently all the feelings that words couldn't come close to expressing. They had come so far together that now they were on unfamiliar ground, taking each moment as it came. Gabe wasn't sure how to act toward her; he was amazed at the depth of intimacy that still shivered between them. On other mornings like this in the long-ago past, he had fought boredom and awkwardness and a frantic urge to be alone. This was so different. He felt passionately, powerfully connected to her.

"If you'd turn the polka music down," he said finally, "you'd hear my heart pounding."

Nothing he could have said would have made her happier. She adjusted the volume, catching her lip between her teeth to try to control her lopsided grin. "I found a new station to listen to," she said. "I know how you feel about waking up to rock music. I thought we'd try something new in the mornings."

Nothing she could have said would have made him happier. "So we wake up to polka music from now on?"

"It's a start."

His breath came in a ragged shiver as he stared at her. The heat from the stove had left a mark like a child's sunburn on her nose and chin. The expression in her clear brown eyes was part child, part temptress. He wanted to spout poetry, to tell her how she had entered his shadow life like sunlight, but instead he blurted out, "I adore you. I love you. I love you so much. I adore you..."

It seemed to convey the message. She closed the distance between them with a cry between a laugh and a sob, throwing herself into his arms with enough force to knock the breath out of him. "I love you, too." She scattered kisses everywhere her lips could reach, his neck, his chin, his ear. "Last night was the best thing that ever happened to me. You're the best thing that ever happened to me. I adore you. Always, always...."

He held her tight, pressing a shaky smile to her hair. "How can you say I'm the best thing that ever happened to you? You don't remember what came before."

She seemed to hesitate, then lifted her head and looked at him. "I know. I know."

There was burned French toast on the counter and more French toast burning on the griddle, but neither of them was thinking about food. They started kissing, openmouthed, ravenous and insatiable. There was no consideration or grace in their movements, they tore at buttons and zippers, making a bed on the hard floor of discarded flannel and denim. In both of them was a frantic compulsion to touch and taste and find, to get closer until they were inside the same skin. Although it had been only a few hours, they coupled like lovers meeting after years of separation. They didn't know who entered whom, they were both completely surrounded and invaded. Every touch triggered memories of shared orgasms, a powerful chain reaction of furious pleasure. They trusted each other with everything they had, but still they found themselves falling, spinning off into a universe of pure, blinding sensation....

The lowly polka, Gabe decided much later, was a vastly underrated dance.

"Forty-year-old men shouldn't have sex on the kitchen floor," Gabe said. "It's undignified."

A.J. smiled at her forty-year-old, undignified lover for all she was worth. They were no longer on the kitchen floor, thank goodness. They were sharing A.J.'s bed, since it was closest to the kitchen. After passion was spent, hardwood became amazingly unromantic. "It's masochistic. I have bruises in places I have never had bruises before."

"I'll be on crutches by noon if you don't leave me alone."

"I have no intention of leaving you alone. A nice hot bath and a deep heat massage and you'll be good as new."

He covered his eyes with his hand, but his wide mouth was quirked in a wry smile. "Oh, for the energy of youth."

She flopped over on her side and punched him in the shoulder. "Stop obsessing about your age, *Mr. Coulter*. I'm beginning to resent it. There aren't that many years between us."

He spread his fingers and uncovered one eye, squinting at her. "Oh, yes? And how do you know that, my precious, foolish love? As far as your memory goes, you're less than a week old."

For a moment, A.J. was unable to speak. She knew she had waited far too long already to tell him the truth. She also knew now was as good a time as any to come clean.

And she *might* have, she really might have found the courage—if they hadn't suddenly been interrupted by an unmistakable, enthusiastic rapping on the front door.

Gabe said an interesting word, tossed off the covers and walked stark naked across the room. "I'll be right back," he said conversationally. "I'm just going to plant my fist in Boyd's face."

"Clothes!" A.J. yelped, sitting bolt upright. "Your pants are on the—"

"Kitchen floor," Gabe said, giving her a look over his shoulder that made her skin burn. "I remember."

A.J. leaned back against the pillows, clutching the crumpled sheet to her chest with a suddenly cold hand. Reality hit her like a slap in the face. Boyd. Dear heaven, why had he come? He'd promised to give her time to tell Gabe the truth. She'd had less than a day. Less than twenty-four hours to know what it was like to be loved for herself. Had that been too much to ask?

She got up and quickly dressed in her silk skirt and blouse. She'd ironed them herself the day before, scorching the fragile material with iron-shaped polka dots. It didn't matter what she looked like. Nothing mattered but what Boyd might be telling Gabe at this very moment. She had to stop him.

They weren't in the kitchen or the living room, but she could hear the slow creaking of the swing on the front porch. An ominous creaking. She flung open the screen door and raced outside in her bare feet, breathing as though she'd just run a marathon.

"Where's the fire?" Gabe inquired mildly. "Been playing with the stove again?"

He was alone on the swing. Bare-chested, with rumpled hair and a strange unfamiliar expression. One foot kept the porch swing idly in motion.

"Where's Boyd?" A.J. blurted, searching the porch, searching the woods, even looking high into the tree house. "Was that Boyd? Where did he go?"

"That was Boyd, we had a little chat, he borrowed my chain saw and left."

His voice. Was it her imagination, or did she detect a grim note in his voice? "He didn't stay long," she said hoarsely.

"No." Gabe stared at her for what felt like an eternity. "Girl clothes. You look like a whole different person, you know that?"

"Oh, Lord," A.J. whispered miserably. He knew. Boyd had ratted on her. How did a woman logically explain away five fiancés? How could she make Gabe understand how the last few days had opened her eyes to the things that were important in life? She wasn't the same person. Everything had changed.

"Sit," Gabe said quietly, sliding over to make room on the swing. "We need to have a serious talk."

Angel Conaught had never been good at "serious talks." She panicked, her eyes skittering away from his. "Aren't you cold without a shirt? That swing is probably wet from the rain—"

"The sun's been up for hours. It's dry. Sit with me."

Helpless, hopeless, she sat down beside him. She stared straight ahead, seeing nothing, frantically wondering where to begin.

But he did it for her, quickly, like a razor slitting straight into her heart. "This isn't easy to say. We should have talked about this long before we came this far."

She looked over at him uneasily. "Gabe, before you—"

He held up his hand. "Just listen. I've been sitting out here trying to figure out the best way to handle this. It's probably the hardest thing I've ever—"

"But I can explain!" She couldn't meet his eyes now, she could only look down at her feet and rub her palms over her knees and try not to choke on the apprehension taking her by the throat. "I swear I didn't know who I was until I saw my photograph in the *Inquisitor* yesterday. I swear I didn't. And I wanted to tell you I was beginning to remember everything, but it felt so good to be here with you, to be this anonymous A.J. person who didn't have to live up or down to anything. I *did* make you happy, so it wasn't so bad to postpone telling you the truth for a little while, was it? Even if you'd never heard of Angel Conaught before, there are plenty of people who have and who would be more than happy to give you an earful. Not that I don't deserve some of it, but...not all of it. I'm only twenty-four years old, I couldn't possibly have done everything I'm accused of—there just hasn't been time. Gabe, I wanted you to know me the way I am now, the way I am with you. That's why I wouldn't let Boyd tell you the truth yesterday when he finally realized who I was. I wanted more time. It wasn't fair to you, I realize that now, but my intentions were good. I didn't realize how much I disliked Angel Conaught until I became someone called A.J. Well, I *wasn't* likable—any of my ex-fiancés will testify to that in court. In fact, Corwin's going to do just that. Anyway, when I started remembering things, I thought maybe it was all meant to be. Corwin following me from L.A. to Denver, the terrible fight we had, my running the car off the road...maybe it was all part of a bigger picture. Maybe it was fate that you were the one who rescued me. I'm still not sure how I ended up underneath the picnic table, but—''

A hand was clamped none-too-gently over her mouth. Gabe's voice was very low and very close to her ear. "What...the...*hell* are you talking about?''

A.J.'s heart stopped. Permanently and forever. She shook off his hand, staring into the light blue eyes just inches from her own. Feeling foolish and debased, knowing she'd jumped off the point of no return with both feet in her mouth, she pressed her trembling lips tightly together. *Doom.*

"I can wait," Gabe said. "I've got all day." For such a soft voice, it had a lot of edges to it.

"He never told you," A.J. muttered wretchedly. "Boyd didn't tell you who I was."

"I told you. Boyd borrowed my chain saw and left."

A.J. felt like she was falling inside her own skin, tumbling down, down, down . . . and she didn't anticipate a happy landing. "Gabe, I was going to tell you everything. Soon. I just . . . didn't know how to start."

"I can help you with that." He leaned forward, resting his arms on his knees, hands dangling between his legs. His back was smooth and tautly muscled, his profile clean, beautiful and expressionless. "Start at the beginning and don't stop until you reach the end. I want to hear everything."

Which she eventually managed to tell him, although she began at the end, babbled in the middle and wound up somewhere at the beginning. The entire uninspiring and embarrassing life story of Angel Jordana Conaught. Gabe listened in a prickly silence, a dark red flush creeping up his neck when she mentioned having had "a few" fiancés.

"Now here's an interesting part." He turned his head slowly sideways, his eyes glittering like sugar crystals. "Just how many is a few, if you don't mind my asking?"

For a moment, she couldn't talk. Her throat burned with tears and frustration. She held up one hand, wiggling all five fingers.

"I don't believe this." He almost smiled, but it wasn't a reassuring smile by any means. "You must have a very low threshold of boredom."

"It was the only time my father ever looked at me." Her hand pressed hard on the base of her throat, as if she could slow her galloping pulse. "The less suitable the fiancé was, the more attention the engagement guaranteed. It was childish and stupid and..." Her voice trailed off miserably as she shook her head. "And so very typical. I told you I didn't like myself very much. I didn't even realize why I did the things I did until my father died unexpectedly a few months ago. By then it was too late to redeem myself. I'd chosen all the wrong ways of trying to connect with him."

"D. Quinn Conaught." Gabe made a dark, moody sound, passing his hand over his eyes. "I've heard of him, of course, but I didn't know he'd passed away. I'm sorry. That must have been hard for you."

"Do you know what the hardest thing was?" Her voice dropped to a hushed whisper, as if she were afraid she would be overheard. "I know this is a terrible thing to say, but...I don't think I really loved my father. I wanted to, but... he was always so cold, so closed off from me. I can't remember him hugging or kissing me, not once. It was so hard to say goodbye to him and know it was final, that there would never be a second chance for us to have any kind of relationship."

"Second chances." Gabe's voice was bleak. "Not many people have second chances in this world. They're kind of like miracles. Nice to think about, but hard to come by."

The worried look on A.J.'s face wavered a bit. He didn't sound angry. He sounded . . . lonely. His head was turned half-away from her, the breeze playing through his long hair with gentle fingers. "Gabe? Now that you know who I am, does it change anything?"

He didn't answer for the longest time. Then he looked straight into her eyes and said flatly, "It changes everything."

A cold fist closed over her stomach. "What do you mean?"

He stood up stiffly, as if every muscle in his body protested the movement. "I mean you're going home where you belong. Today."

A.J. moved with a jerk on the swing, like someone had touched her with a live wire. "You don't mean that," she said through a dry throat.

He stood silent, his thumbs hooked into the pockets of his jeans.

A.J. touched his thigh with shaking fingers. "You're angry with me and I don't blame you, but you have to remember something. No matter what my name is, no matter where I come from or what I've done, I'm still the same woman you fell in love with."

He moved abruptly, out of her reach. "And I'm still the same man you fell in love with. Which makes this whole damn thing . . ." He shook his head, giving the sky a bitter smile. "Hell, I must have been crazy. To think I actually let myself believe . . ."

A.J. was lost. She stood up, her whole body shaking. There was a drowning sensation washing over her, a nauseating feeling of helplessness and disbelief. "Gabe, you're scaring me. You believed what I believed, and it's still true. What we have is real. What we have is a future."

"A future?" He laughed then, and the sound seemed to echo all through the trees and sky. "What we have is *over*. I'll take you into town as soon as I'm dressed."

"You don't mean this!" she cried. "Damn it, what are you trying to do, punish me? I said I was sorry. I should have told you who I was yesterday. *I'm sorry!*"

He lifted both fists and knuckled his eyes, the gesture reminiscent of an exhausted child who had been crying. But when he looked at her, his eyes were dry. "And I should have told you who I was," he said simply, quietly. "And what I was."

Then, moving like a sleepwalker, he went inside the house.

Doc Hornbaker found A.J. curled up on the swing fifteen minutes later. She hadn't heard him drive up the lane; she didn't even see him until he stood directly in front of her.

"Company's calling," he announced cheerfully, wriggling his bushy brows. "And a darned attractive fellow it is."

A.J. blinked up at him with gritty, red-rimmed eyes. The doctor took a good long look at her face and lost his smile.

"Damn, damn, *damn* that fool Gabe Coulter," he said. "When I was out here the other day, I couldn't help but notice Mother Nature clicking between you two. I'd figured everything would turn out just fine, but I should have known better. No, sir, Gabe never makes anything easy on himself or anyone else. Should I go in there and punch his lights out for making you miserable? It would probably do him a world of good."

It was a blustery threat designed more to cheer her up than anything else, but A.J. couldn't have smiled to save her life.

"He doesn't want me," she said helplessly. "Now that I'm me . . . he doesn't want me."

Now one bushy brow arched high while the other lowered in fierce concentration. "Come again?"

"He doesn't want me here anymore. He's sending me home."

"You don't know where home is, child."

"I do now." Her voice was tiny and glum. "I wish I didn't. I was happier when I didn't know who I was. He was happier. Everything was wonderful. Now that I know who I am . . . he says I don't know who *he* is. He says it's over. It doesn't make sense. I don't know what to do. I can't think. My feet are cold."

Doc Hornbaker took off his woolly cardigan and tucked it around her feet on the swing. "I don't understand a word of what you're saying, but I don't want you worrying. You just be patient here and I'll go have a talk with Gabe. I can just about promise you everything is all his fault. He's a stubborn son of a bitch—uh, excuse me, that wasn't what I meant to say.

He can be difficult at times, but he has a heart of gold. At least I think he does, the stubborn son of... well, sit tight, why don't you? Just sit tight while I sort this out." He marched over to the screen door and threw it open with a bang, then turned back to A.J. "You say you remembered who you are? When did this happen?"

"Yesterday," she said listlessly. "Bits and pieces at first, then... everything."

"Well, that's wonderful. Now you can tell me your proper name."

"Angel."

"Angel." Doc Hornbaker sighed and wagged his head. "A sweet girl like you with a beautiful name like that... and he made you cry. That man inside should be ashamed of himself."

Ten

Gabe had told A.J.—Angel—that he was going to get dressed and drive her into town. Instead, he went to his room and sat down on his bed, his hands closed tight over the edge of the mattress. The sheets were still tangled in lovers' knots from the night before. The faint, sweet smell of lovemaking still lingered in the air.

He was a fool.

This wasn't the first time in his life he had faced the fact, but it was by far the most painful. This morning he had allowed himself to believe in a fairy tale. A.J. would never leave him. She would be content here. She would sit with him by the fire at night and play Scrabble. He would teach her to fish. He would show her the fine art of cooking on a gas stove without burning the house down. They would take long walks in the springtime and he would tuck wildflowers into her hair. He could almost hear the sad violins weeping.

The facts were, Angel Conaught was sixteen years younger than he was and about a billion dollars richer. He was a damn *retiree* for all intents and purposes.

And that wasn't all he was.

This hurt so much, losing everything he had all over again. What had happened to his tough hide, to that protective turtle shell he'd grown in the past two years? He felt raw, all his nerve endings exposed on the surface of his skin. His stomach wrenched and burned, doubling him in two. Love and bleeding ulcers. For Gabe Coulter, it was like night and day. One inevitably followed the other.

"I ought to box your ears."

Gabe groaned, looking at Archie's massive bulk filling his doorway. "Hell. Someone should have told me this was Ruin Gabe Coulter's Life day. Come on in, Archie, box my ears. It'll take my mind off my stomach."

The doctor in Archie took over. Temporarily. "Ulcer?"

"No, Archie," Gabe shot back sarcastically. "Just a little upset tummy. Yes, it's my damned ulcer. It feels like Vesuvius is erupting in there."

He didn't deserve any sympathy, Archie decided. He was too damned belligerent. "Well, you reap what you sow. I just talked to that wet-nosed woman outside, and I'll tell you something. You've got her half out of her mind with worry. She thinks you don't care about her."

"I'm sending her home. That's the kindest thing I can do for her."

"Call me stupid, but I don't think she feels the same way." Archie paused, distracted by a sudden thought. "Where is her home, by the way?"

"Los Angeles. That wet-nosed woman out there is named Angel Conaught, and she's worth more money than you and I and everyone else in Colorado put together."

"So what's your point?" Archie demanded.

Gabe rolled his eyes. "Never mind. Forget it. Why do I bother trying to hold conversations with you?"

"Hell if I know. It's not like you ever listen to me." Archie glared at him, hitching up his pants in a fighting gesture. "Well, you're going to listen this time. You and I both know damn well why you're acting like a jackass."

Gabe narrowed his eyes. "What do you mean, acting like a—"

"Quiet!" Archie bellowed. "I'm on a roll here. You pay attention and maybe you'll learn something. When you came here two years ago, you were the sorriest sight I'd ever seen. I helped you because I'd never seen a man more determined to put his mistakes behind him. And you did it, damn it all, you saved yourself, and it's something you should be proud of." Then, in a different tone of voice, he added, "She doesn't know, does she? You're hiding it. You didn't tell her."

"That I was flat-on-my-face drunk for seven years?" Gabe dropped his head in his hands. "No,

Archie. It's not something we chatted about over breakfast.''

"You talk like you were a miserable failure. You weren't. You were the best damn trial attorney on the East Coast."

"That I was." Gabe's voice was muffled and bitter. "I never lost a case, not once. That's why I stayed more or less sober during the day. I had this dazzling reputation to uphold. Guilty or innocent, if Gabe Coulter defended you, you didn't have a worry in the world. Except maybe how to pay his astronomical fees."

Archie's back was to the door, Gabe's head was hanging nearly to his knees. Neither of them noticed A.J. standing in the doorway.

"You're too hard on yourself," Archie said quietly. "You always have been, in my opinion. You did some good things."

"And I did some bad things," Gabe replied. "And those were the things I found a little hard to live with. It's a good thing I had the bottle to ease my conscience, isn't it?"

"That's over. You have your whole life ahead of you."

Gabe smiled without humor, looking up at his friend. "I already had my big chance at making my mark in the world, and I blew it. What do you want me to do? Get down on my knees and ask a woman like A.J. to stay here in the middle of nowhere with a pathetic has-been? She's got the world at her feet, literally. I'm not going to expect..." He stopped abruptly, his gaze locking with A.J.'s over Archie's shoulder. She looked so calm, so beautiful, no trace of revulsion or sympathy on her face. And for once, much older than her years.

"Damn it all," he whispered, straight from the heart.

A.J. walked slowly into the room, touching Archie on the shoulder. "Could I please talk to Gabe alone?"

Archie looked from one pale face to the other. "I wish you luck. The man is difficult, but I don't believe he's hopeless."

After Archie left them, Gabe felt at a distinct disadvantage sitting on the bed. He tried to stand, but his ulcer protested with white-hot fury.

"Why didn't you tell me you had an ulcer?" A.J. asked softly.

Gabe doubled over, clenching his teeth until the pain subsided. "I thought it was under control. It *was* under control, until..."

"Until me." A.J. hesitated, then sat down beside him on the bed. Her hands were folded prayer-style in her lap. "You haven't been any more honest with me than I've been with you."

"I suppose not." He couldn't look at her.

"No." They said nothing for a moment, then A.J. gave his ulcer another nasty shock by saying quietly, "Will you marry me, Mr. Coulter?"

"Damn it!" This time Gabe managed to get to his feet. "Damn it, what's the matter with you? Didn't you hear what I just told Archie? I'm an *alcoholic*. I keep that bottle of bourbon on my fireplace mantel to remind me just how vulnerable I am. A small thing, but it was big enough to destroy my life and my career. Actually, I don't know what took me down first, my ego or the alcohol, but it doesn't matter. I'm no prize."

"Neither am I," A.J. said thoughtfully. "I'm a selfish, vain, misguided, self-pitying spoiled brat. With all I had, I never knew what it was to be happy until I came here. And I never knew what it was to care more for someone else than I did for myself until I fell in love with you. I'm certainly no prize."

Gabe began pacing, slightly stooped, one arm held hard over his stomach. "I have a news flash for you. You're bright and beautiful and funny and you have your entire life ahead of you. Go home where you belong and start living it."

She looked up at him curiously. "Why don't you?"

"Why don't I what?"

"Start living your life again."

He stopped pacing, staring at her with brooding eyes. "I am living, baby. This is it for me. I belong here. I don't need money or excitement or a constant high for my ego. I passed that stage a long time ago. I found what I was looking for right here."

She stood up, taking a deep breath. "Yourself?" she guessed tonelessly. "That's what you're telling me? You came here to find yourself?"

"That's right."

"You're a liar." Suddenly her voice began to shake. "You didn't find yourself here, Gabe Coulter. You'll never find yourself here, and do you know why? You didn't *lose* yourself here. You got lost somewhere else a long time ago. You're just hiding out here, passing the time."

"Now she's a shrink!" he shouted to the room at large. "Still wet behind the ears, and she thinks she knows it all. Let me enlighten you, Sigmund Freud. A few years ago when I was riding high on my success, I agreed to defend the son of a congressman who'd been accused of armed robbery. You know why I took the case? Two reasons—it was big news and it was big money. And I did it, I got my client acquitted on a technicality. Two months later the same kid was arrested for robbing a convenience store. The owner was killed in that little fiasco."

She was silent for a moment. Her face was strained. "So you started drinking."

"No, I started drinking *more*. But the guilt didn't stop me from practicing law, and the law didn't stop me from serving my own needs. Not until two years ago when I finally realized I was killing myself. One day I just walked out of my office and never went back. That was the end."

She took a deep breath, then slowly let it out. "It sounds more like a beginning to me."

"Sometimes I forget what a child you are." The words were low and scornful. "Go home, A.J. Fiancé number six is out there waiting for you to find him. There's no time to waste."

"I want to be your wife," she said calmly, as if she hadn't heard a word he'd said. "I want to live with you and grow old with you and make you laugh every single day of our lives, but I won't help you hide. I won't hurt you like that."

"One of us is crazy," Gabe said, desperation and pain forming a haze inside his head. "And one of us is not paying attention to what the other is saying. I didn't ask you to marry me.''

"You want to marry me," she said simply. "I'm the best thing that's happened to you in a long time. Do you think I don't know how lonely you were before I came? Do you think I don't know how happy I've made you?"

"Happy?" Gabe winced as he heard from his angry ulcer again. "Kiddo, you've got more of an ego than I ever had, and that's saying something."

"No, I'm just being practical. It's my new motto— Be A Practical Person. I've never been too good at it in the past, but a few things have happened lately that make me think I have potential. I can drive a car—sort of—and I can light a gas stove and I can design a tree house and I can make a stubborn, lonely, self-condemning recluse smile any time I want to. That's a start."

The stillness that came over him was so complete, she thought he might have stopped breathing.

"That's enough," he said softly, his lips barely moving. "Go home. You don't belong in Gopher, Angel Conaught."

"Ophir." She held his eyes and held her ground, five-feet-two inches of terrifying blond determination. "And I think you're right, Mr. Coulter. I don't belong here any more than you do. It's a beautiful place to visit, but a very bad place to hide. And call me A.J.''

Something felt like it was dying inside of him. It wasn't his ulcer—no, that was thriving. It was something bright and hopeful inside his soul, something barely acknowledged. "You don't know what the hell you're talking about."

She frowned at him. "Are you sure you were a good lawyer? If that's the best line you can come up with in a pressure-filled situation—"

"I was a bloody unbelievable lawyer!"

"If you say so." She shrugged and moved toward the door, chin in the air and shoulders squared. Her heart was breaking; he'd never know what it cost her not to throw her arms around him and beg him to come with her. She felt like she was turning her back on the Garden of Eden and heading out alone into the cold, cruel world. She believed in Gabe Coulter with all her heart, but that wasn't enough. He had to trust in himself as well, or he ran the risk of going through the rest of his life an emotional cripple. "I want to thank you for looking after me. I love you with all my heart, and I hope you're completely miserable without me. I've decided to go home, after all. As long as Doc Hornbaker is here, I'll ask him to give me a lift back to town. If you ever decide to come looking for me, I live in Laguna Niguel, just outside Los Angeles. There are things I need to do, decisions I have to make that I've been putting off. I think it's time."

And at that moment, Gabe Coulter had a glimpse of the woman A.J. would someday become, the woman she was already well on her way to being. Determined, stubborn and indomitable, yet innocent enough to throw out all the glaring obstacles between them in favor of dreams and optimism.

Dear Lord, how he loved her.

"A.J.?"

She paused in the doorway, hope and hopelessness tearing at her. "What?"

"I'm sorry. I wish I could give you what you deserve."

She blinked away scalding tears, willing herself not to cry. "And what do you think I deserve?"

He closed his eyes briefly. "Someone who saved the very best of himself for you. Someone you could believe in."

"I already found him." She turned away, because the tears were coming after all, and she didn't want him to see. "And now I'm going home to wait for him."

Gabe's expression was bleak. She was so young; he couldn't expect her to understand. "Don't waste your time, A.J., I'm not worth it."

"I guess that's something I'll have to find out for myself. Goodbye, Mr. Coulter."

Eleven

———

"Look out there, to the left of the fountain. The tree—have you ever seen anything like it?"

"So that's the famous sculpture. Someone told me she'd brought the artist over from Europe to do it."

"It does have a European flair. Subtle, with a certain joyful innocence."

"It's quite interesting. Trust Angel Conaught to set a trend. She's fearless, she really is."

"Speaking of fearless, have you met George Marchand's new wife? She's forty years younger if she's a day, and she used to be a *gymnast*. Come inside, I'll introduce you."

A.J. stayed in the shadows of the veranda, waiting until the laughing, gossiping couple strolled back inside the house. She didn't recognize them. Of course, she wasn't personally acquainted with most of the people she was playing hostess to tonight. The guest list had been compiled by her secretary, consisting largely of the executives of Conaught Industries. The party had been given at the suggestion of Dwight Schuller, one of her father's good friends and Conaught's executive vice president. A gathering like this was a dead bore, but it was necessary for morale, he claimed. They were advertising a smooth transition of power from father to daughter, a solid foundation for business as usual. A.J. was painfully aware that her business acumen was sadly lacking. In the past three months, she had sought out trustworthy advice and tried to stay in the background as much as possible. She had no grand master plan to take over where her father had left off; she was more than happy to assume the role of figurehead while her education progressed. Watching her efforts, the hierarchy of Conaught Industries had breathed a collective sigh, daring to voice the hope that Angel Conaught had something upstairs, after all.

It was a cool night. For the most part, the guests made themselves at home in their hostess's thirty-six room mansion and the overwhelmed hostess hid out on the terrace. Seeking the peace and isolation she had craved so often lately, A.J. ran down the veranda steps, lifting her narrow skirt as she darted among pillars and statues and lush green hedges recently trimmed in the shapes of leaping rabbits. This, of course, had been a tribute to the wit and wisdom of Dr. Archie Hornbaker. Whenever she looked at the fanciful hedges, she had to smile. Deep in a garden of luxurious California flora and foliage, a custom-made six-foot marble cherub held a carved plaque high above his curly head: The Main Obligation Is To Amuse Yourself.

But it wasn't the marble cherub or even the leaping green rabbits that had attracted the attention and admiration of the two party-goers on the veranda. There was another new addition to the estate, something A.J. had wanted as long as she could remember. High in the massive branches of a hundred-year-old live oak tree was the most creative, most glorious tree house in all of California.

Granted, there *was* another tree house that rivaled this one, but it was in the state of Colorado. Far, far away in Colorado.

Her heart grew heavy in her chest, just as it always did when her thoughts drifted back to a town called Ophir, to the man with the most beautiful eyes she had ever seen in her life. It seemed like a dozen years ago, it seemed like yesterday.

After three months, she still waited, looking for his face in every room she entered, listening for the husky sound of his voice. Every man she met paled in comparison. Gabe Coulter dominated in every way. He wouldn't let her forget him, he wouldn't let her move on. The vivid memories kept her dangling on a string, waiting and hoping, hoping and waiting.

And still he didn't come.

She wandered over to the old oak, head tipped back to admire her efforts. She'd done a fine job here. It had taken her almost two weeks to build this house from start to finish, and not a soul had helped her.

Some people might look at this tree house and see a floor that wasn't level, or the occasional spaces between the pine boards, or the thousand-plus nails she had hammered in crookedly. But A.J., like the two discriminating party-goers on the veranda earlier, recognized it as a work of art. Gabe would have been proud of her if he could see it. Of course, she wouldn't mention the time she fell out of the tree, bloodying her nose and twisting her ankle. If he was here.

Which he wasn't.

"Damn," she whispered softly, fingering the wooden steps nailed up the side of the tree. She closed her eyes and lost herself in the warm memories of his lovemaking, remembering the fragrance of his skin, the wonderful feel of his hair running through her fingers, his husky, hypnotic voice. And then she pictured his face as she had last seen it, so tight and distant and sad. A long moment passed before she opened her eyes. If there was such a thing as a miracle, he would have been standing here in front of her. But miracles and second chances were hard to come by in this world; she had it on the best authority.

Over and over during the past three months she told herself, You can be anything you want, you can do anything you want. But it was so hard when the heavy, dull shadow of missing him never truly left her. Each and every morning she woke with a numbing surprise that Gabe wasn't with her. It was all so wrong. She felt like Goldilocks, searching for a bed that wasn't too hard or soft, a chair that wasn't too big or small. But nothing truly fit, nothing felt . . . just right. She was determined to be tough, but there were times when she was overwhelmed with the urge to get out of her own body, to just escape somewhere....

Without consciously making the decision, she kicked off her shoes, hitched up the skirt of her white sequined evening gown in one hand and tested the first wooden step with her foot. Yes, she ought to be able to manage this without getting a bloody nose, even in a designer dress that fit like a second skin. And for some reason, she wanted nothing more at the moment than to sit in her very own, custom-built tree house—subtle, but with a certain joyful innocence.

Fortunately, her skirt was slit high up one side, giving her needed room to stretch. She didn't give a thought to the fact that the floodlights in the garden clearly illuminated her unorthodox and unladylike climb up the steps and over the side of the railing. This Angel still... wasn't.

The view was magnificent. She settled back on a long cushion appropriated from one of the lounge chairs by the pool. Music and laughter drifted from the house, tingling on the night air. *It sounded like a lovely party,* she thought with a puckish smile. She hoped her anonymous guests were enjoying it.

"You should be spanked."

It was incredible how the sound of a certain voice could take the wind out of a person. A voice that came from far below her... but not so far away as Colorado. Emotion flooded through her body, filling her up, spilling over, drenching her.

Her lungs waited for the next breath until she was sure. Slowly she leaned her face over the side of the tree house, peering down like a stunned owl. He was looking right back up at her, a beautiful, living, breathing miracle. His sensual, strong-limbed body looked strangely overdecorated in dark slacks and a soft white sweater.

Mr. Coulter.

"You got your hair cut," she croaked.

"And you're wearing pink lacy underwear." Cast in light and shadow, the stark lines of his face were blessedly familiar. "Very nice underwear, but I'm glad I was the one standing below you."

"So am I," she whispered, pressing her shaking fingers to her mouth. "Oh, so am I."

He pushed his hands deep into the pockets of his slacks, the smooth material shaping his lean hips. It was an endearing gesture of a man not entirely sure of his next move. "I would have dressed up a little if I'd known I was party crashing."

"You are dressed up," A.J. said, her eyes shimmering like sequins. "You have shiny shoes on."

His smile was rueful and uncertain and very human. "They're new." Then, so softly she could barely hear, "You're too far away. I'm coming up."

Oh, Lordy... here they were without warning, the tears she had saved up for three whole months. They came like a flash flood, streaming down her face, getting in her nose and mouth. She huddled back against the tree, wiping her cheeks with the back of her hand, wondering if her makeup was all over her face, wondering if she was dreaming, wondering if this meant what she prayed it did.

And knowing deep in her heart the wait was over.

Then he was hunched down beside her, ducking his head to avoid a low-hanging branch, mopping her wet face with his bare hands. "Don't cry. Honey, please don't cry. Everything's going to be all right, it really is. I wouldn't be here if I wasn't sure of that."

A.J. grabbed fistfuls of his sweater and buried her face against his chest. "I've always been sure. What took you so long?"

"Sometimes when you get lost…it takes a while to find yourself again." He squeezed her shoulders, rubbed her back. "I'm working again. I went into partnership with a friend in Los Angeles. Corporate law, mostly. A.J., little love, you're going to hurt yourself if you keep crying like that."

"I c-can't help it," she sobbed. "I have all this loneliness and frustration all b-b-bottled up in me."

"Baby, I'm so sorry." He pulled back, taking her face between his hands and looking down at her. She was striped with mascara and tears, the rhythm of her breathing hectic and uncontrolled. She was the most beautiful second chance he had ever seen in his life. "I never wanted to hurt you, but I had to be sure. I had to know you would be safe with me."

A.J. shuddered, her sobs decreasing as she realized the enormity of the step he had taken. She had been so certain he needed to confront his past to be free, but what if she was wrong? Had she pushed him too far? He had worked so hard to find a measure of peace in his life; she didn't want to take that away from him. "I don't want to hurt you, either. I just want you to be happy. If I was wrong, if this is going to be too hard for you—"

"This is scary as hell," he admitted softly. Then he gave her a sudden, rueful smile. "Almost as scary as all these beautiful people in that cozy little mansion of yours. Did you know they all have perfect teeth and perfect tans and perfect hair? I noticed that when I was wandering around looking for you. So much perfection gathered together in one place. No wonder you escaped to your tree house."

"I built it myself." Her troubled expression changed. "*It's* not perfect."

"Perfection is overrated. Will you learn to fish?"

A smile broke through, just as he hoped. "M-maybe."

"Then I'll make you French toast every morning for breakfast and I'll let you wear my clothes any time you want and I'll make a beautiful wooden cradle for our first-born child with my own two hands. Cradles are supposed to rock, so I have an advantage. Everything I make rocks."

She was laughing now. "I know. I'm sorry."

He kissed her, long and deep. Against the corner of her mouth he whispered, "Don't be sorry. Don't be sorry about anything, ever, ever again. I love you. I swear I will keep you safe and cherish you as long as I live."

"But I've got all this *money*..." A.J. groaned, as if it were a major drawback. Which she truly believed it was.

"I know. I'm too old for you and you have too much money, I make rocking kitchen tables and you have terrible taste in music. I have an ulcer and you cry too much. That's just life. We'll muddle through."

Dear Mr. Coulter, who was always so good at cutting through to the simple heart of the matter. Her love for him was the purest, most intense emotion she had ever experienced. The fact that he was willing to face his demons for her meant more than she could put into words. She'd never been that important before, not to anyone.

"I'll take care of you, too," she whispered. "We'll take care of each other."

His finger slowly traced the heart-shaped neckline of her gown. His mouth hovered over hers. "You look like an angel in that dress."

She touched his upper lip with the tip of her tongue. "You look like a lawyer with that haircut."

"I am a lawyer. A damn good one."

"Well, I'm no angel."

His voice had a ragged edge as he asked, "What are you doing?"

"Proving it. Can we go to Gopher for our honeymoon?"

"*Ophir.* We can't do this in a tree house. There's no way... there's just no... oh, that feels good. You feel so good..."

"So do you, Mr. Coulter."

"Call me Gabe," he said.

*   *   *   *   *

It takes a very special man to win

She's friend, wife, mother—she's you! And beside each Special Woman stands a wonderfully *special* man. It's a celebration of our heroines—and the men who become part of their lives.

Look for these exciting titles from Silhouette Special Edition:

January **BUILDING DREAMS** by Ginna Gray

February **HASTY WEDDING** by Debbie Macomber

March **THE AWAKENING** by Patricia Coughlin

April **FALLING FOR RACHEL** by Nora Roberts

Dont miss THAT SPECIAL WOMAN! each month—from your special authors.

AND

For the most special woman of all—you, our loyal reader—we have a wonderful gift: a beautiful journal to record all of your special moments. See this month's THAT SPECIAL WOMAN! title for details.

TSW1

For all those readers who've been looking for something a little bit different, a little bit spooky, let Silhouette Books take you on a journey to the dark side of love with

SILHOUETTE
Shadows
™

If you like your romance mixed with a hint of danger, a taste of something eerie and wild, you'll love Shadows. This new line will send a shiver down your spine and make your heart beat faster. It's full of romance and more—and some of your favorite authors will be featured right from the start. Look for our four launch titles wherever books are sold, because you won't want to miss a single one.

THE LAST CAVALIER—Heather Graham Pozzessere
WHO IS DEBORAH?—Elise Title
STRANGER IN THE MIST—Lee Karr
SWAMP SECRETS—Carla Cassidy

After that, look for two books every month, and prepare to tremble with fear—and passion.

SILHOUETTE SHADOWS, coming your way in March.

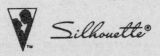

Silhouette®

SHAD1

Take 4 bestselling love stories FREE

Plus get a FREE surprise gift!

**Silhouette Books
is proud to present
our best authors,
their best books...
and the best in
your reading pleasure!**

Throughout 1993, look for exciting books
by these top names in contemporary
romance:

CATHERINE COULTER—
Aftershocks in February

FERN MICHAELS—
Whisper My Name in March

DIANA PALMER—
Heather's Song in March

ELIZABETH LOWELL—
Love Song for a Raven in April

SANDRA BROWN
(previously published under
the pseudonym Erin St. Claire)—
Led Astray in April

LINDA HOWARD—
All That Glitters in May

When it comes to passion,
we wrote the book.

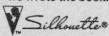

BOBT1R

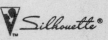